"I can't believe my good fortune, finding you again after all these years," Allen confessed.

I still love you, he thought.

"I've been here all along. Or almost all that time." Maureen gave him a small smile.

Their eyes met across the length of the sofa. Moments later, he slid across the sofa and caught her in the curve of his arm. He sat there without talking, holding her gently.

More than anything he wanted to lean down and kiss her. Instead, he kissed the top of her head.

"I've made plans for us on Saturday, if you can get away. How about cycling along the coast?"

"Like we used to?"

So she remembered. He cupped her chin. "Are you free?"

"Yes, I have no obligations." She gazed up at him. "Allen, you look troubled. Have you forgotten how to ride a bike?"

"No." But I'd almost forgotten how much you once meant to me, he realized.

DORIS ELAINE FELL

With books and dolls as her companions, Doris knew from the time she was seven that she wanted to be a nurse and a writer when she grew up. Challenged by these childhood dreams, she escaped the confinement of a tiny hometown to pursue a multifaceted career as a teacher, missionary, nurse, freelance editor and author. Her diverse professions have taken her to a Carib village in Guatemala, a Swiss chalet in the Alps, through rugged mountain passes in Mexico, and to a bamboo schoolhouse in the Philippines. She also thoroughly enjoys her teddy bear collection and sitting by the river in eastern Washington with her great-nieces and nephews.

But it was as a high schooler that Doris knelt by her bedside and asked God for the privilege of one day writing for His glory. For the past nine years she has written full-time, expressing her love for a gracious God and her love of life and living. As evident in *Long-Awaited Wedding,* her first romance novel with Steeple Hill, the subtle theme of forgiveness marks her writing. Other publishers of her work include Crossway Books and Fleming Revell. She is currently under contract for her fifteenth book.

Long-Awaited Wedding
Doris Elaine Fell

Love Inspired

Published by Steeple Hill Books™

STEEPLE HILL BOOKS

Steeple
Hill™

ISBN 0-373-87062-0

LONG-AWAITED WEDDING

Copyright © 1999 by Doris Elaine Fell

Look us up on-line at: http://www.steeplehill.com

Printed in U.S.A.

Search me, O God, and know my heart;
test me and know my anxious thoughts.
See if there is any offensive way in me,
and lead me in the way everlasting.
—*Psalm* 139:23-24

To

HANNAH MARIE

WHO WANTS TO BE A WIFE AND MOMMY
WHEN SHE GROWS UP

Chapter One

Maureen Davenport entered the restaurant on the arm of Dwayne Crocker, an affable, rangy man in his late thirties, a brilliant engineer with a genius for math, a drolly humorous man…a total bore. She wondered now why she had agreed to come with him.

She had planned on leaving work on time and heading straight home for a relaxing soak in the hot tub. It was her way to unravel, to close out the day, to shut out her anxieties over the pending merger between Fabian Industries and Larhaven Aircraft. Her preoccupation with the merger had left her without defense or excuses when Dwayne blocked her exit at closing time and asked, "How about dinner and a show this evening?"

So here she was, sitting across from him in a crowded restaurant that smelled of fried chicken and wondering how she could endure five hours in Dwayne's company. She had expected this type of place—an economical menu with a quaint old-fashioned setting, tables crowded together and an abundance of fussing children.

She ran her hand over the closed menu, deciding on

the house salad and a steaming cup of tea. Idly she watched Dwayne adjust his silver-rimmed glasses. The glasses magnified the glossy gray of his eyes—his best feature—and now as she met his glance, she saw the flecks of dark blue in the gray. His dancing eyes were evenly set in his narrow face, a not unpleasant face in spite of the prominent bony structure.

Before she could tell him what she wanted, he turned to the waitress, arched his thick brows and said, "We're starving. Make it two chicken dinners—the whole works. Tea for the lady—"

So he remembered her preference, she thought.

"And coffee for me. And bring plenty of biscuits."

As they waited, he knuckled his fingers. "Did I blow it?"

She mellowed her response. "I only wanted a salad."

"And some place more exclusive?" He pulled a candle from his pocket and shoved it in the flower vase. Then he whipped out a lighter and made a ceremony of lighting it. "There, is that better?" he asked.

The flickering flame caught the light in his eyes again. "Do you always carry candles in your pocket, Dwayne?"

"Your secretary told me you like candlelight and fancy restaurants in Los Angeles or Newport. But getting a reservation this late—well, actually I didn't bother. We'd miss the show."

The show. Maureen had momentarily forgotten the theater. She moved her arm as the waitress set the rhubarb and house salad in front of her and put a plate of hot biscuits on the table.

"Maureen, are you married?" Dwayne asked.

She stared him down. "Dwayne, if I were married I would not be having dinner with you."

He glanced at the opal ring on her left hand. "Don't take offense. I've asked around and no one seems to know anything about your life outside of the office."

"That's the way I like it."

At thirty-seven, Maureen was a poised, confident woman. Men often commented on her stunning appearance and her stylish clothes. Her good looks and social skills had helped her, but she'd managed to climb the ladder of success mainly through her intellect and sheer hard work. She had earned respect and equal footing with the men she worked with. But she was still a private person, her life outside Fabian strictly her own.

She said guardedly, "I was married once to Carl Davenport."

She had met Carl in Indianapolis, where she worked right out of graduate school. He was wealthy and charming, witty and handsome, a superb dancer. Carl had liked his music fast and his tempo of living even faster.

She sighed. "Perhaps you've heard of my husband—Carl drove the Indianapolis 500."

"Carl Davenport?" Excitement brightened Dwayne's ordinary features. "I would never have guessed—"

An awkward pause cut his sentence short. He met her gaze and then said quietly, "He was killed driving the Indy 500, wasn't he?"

"Yes, five years ago. His car crashed and burned." She shivered, and felt the fine hairs on her arm curl. They had been on the verge of real happiness—of working out their differences. She felt her lips pinch. "He was only thirty-two when he died."

"Too young."

She smiled wanly. "He was doing what he liked doing best."

"Yeah, I guess you can look at it that way. So you've

been married and widowed. That's a well kept secret at the office."

Over the years, Maureen had kept another secret. Whatever you do, Dwayne Crocker, she warned silently, don't ask me if Carl and I had children. I would have to lie and I have denied my daughter long enough.

Even as she looked across the table at Dwayne, Maureen remained calm, the thudding of her heart not visible to him. But surely he would think it was Carl's child, not Allen's. No one knew of the birth of Allen's child, given up for adoption nineteen years ago. Almost twenty. Maureen rarely allowed herself to dwell on the infant daughter she had given away. And yet the girl was always there in Maureen's mind. In her heart. In her dreams. In this restaurant filled with strangers.

"Any kids, Maureen?"

"One daughter," she said, and then quickly asked, "And you, Dwayne, have you ever been married?"

"I'm still waiting for the right girl to come along."

Don't wait too long, she thought. You're pushing forty.

But what did she want? She had no immediate plans to remarry again and settle down. She would if the right person came along, but for now she was carving out her niche in the business world.

But what if the "right man" came along? She knew for certain that Dwayne Crocker was not the one. As he talked on, she did what she always did when she sat across the table from a boring dinner date—she imagined that "special" person sitting there. Allen was always the right one, but he was gone, presumably lost in one of the country's peacekeeping missions. After all these years, it was like lighting an old torch, like awakening a sleeping giant, like plucking back a painful memory.

She tried to picture Allen across the table from her—older, wiser, handsome. Smiling and leaning forward and boasting that his father was grooming him to take over the family dynasty.

"So what do you think?" Dwayne's question cut into her thoughts.

"Excuse me?" Maureen asked, embarrassed to have drifted off.

"I just suggested that you run away with me to some far-off island and get married."

She laughed. "You do know how to get a woman's attention."

Maureen was thankful when their waitress arrived with fried chicken, mashed potatoes with country gravy, and biscuits with honey. She ate more than she had intended, as Dwayne monopolized the conversation.

He was unstoppable, inexhaustible, talking figures through much of the dinner. The billions of dollars of government overspending and predictions for the Dow Jones averages. Then—just when she thought that he was running out of steam—he offered statistics that would iron out the flaws in the Fabian missile project. He was right, too. Dwayne Crocker didn't make mistakes.

Normally she might find his conversation stimulating. But tonight the information seemed wearying, irksome, oppressive.

As the last roll disappeared from his plate, Dwayne carefully licked the honey from his finger. Over steaming cups of coffee and tea, he discussed the financial advantages of merging. He favored the merger with Larhaven.

She dreaded it.

"It's nothing but a hostile takeover," she said hotly.

"But, Maureen, Larhaven will come out on the winning side. Once we combine building military aircraft and the skins of commercial liners and keep signing contracts for more missiles, there's no stopping us."

"I dislike the bidding wars," she told him.

"Look, a merger means billions of dollars on the drawing board. Fabian can't keep pace with the industry unless we merge."

But it wasn't fair to be so close to being CEO at Fabian and then lose out to a merger, she thought. She'd never have another opportunity to move to the top. "Jobs will be slashed," she reminded Dwayne. "Hundreds of them. I expected to replace Eddie McCormick when he retired. Now I don't even know whether I'll have a job at all."

"You know why McCormick stayed on? He's fishing for better dollar signs and benefits in his retirement package. But my job's secure," Dwayne boasted. "They need my mathematical genius."

"I wouldn't count on it. Larhaven will bring in their own management team."

He looked surprised. "No chance they'll let me go. If they do, I head right to their competitor. They won't let you go either, Maureen. They may not want women as vice-presidents, but they will need research scientists."

He pushed his plate aside and told the waitress to bring two apple pies. "Why are you so worried, Maureen? What did you do—have a run-in with the powers that be at Larhaven?"

"A long time ago. Old man Kladis doesn't favor women on his board."

"He's been dead for ten years. His eldest son runs the show."

Her body went rigid. *Allen Kladis?* "I thought Allen was dead," she said softly.

"No, his wife died. About a year ago. But Allen is still going strong. He's the force behind this merger. I can't believe you. Haven't you been listening in the conference room? Eddie keeps talking about A. G. Kladis. The guy's about my age."

Allen's age.

So Allen was the head of Larhaven, not the father? What was his father's name? Adam? No, Alexander G. Kladis, a tall man with olive skin and a barrel chest and anger in his black eyes, a father who had been determined to make millionaires out of his three boys even if he had to stomp on the heart of a seventeen-year-old girl who loved his eldest son more than anything else in the world.

"Maureen, are you all right? You look sick."

"I have a headache. I just need to get some air."

Dwayne dropped a tip on the table as they stood.

He gave her a winsome smile as they left the table. "Can we have dinner again soon, Maureen?"

She smiled back. "I'm too full to think about it right now."

"Then I'll keep asking."

As they reached the door he gently touched her elbow. "Maureen, I've apparently given you a shock. I'm sorry. But when you get back to the office tomorrow, read the correspondence—check the masthead on the Larhaven contract. A. G. Kladis is CEO at Larhaven."

Allen Kladis, not his father Alexander. She felt a stinging betrayal. Alexander Kladis had won. Why had the older Kladis lied to her so long ago? Why had he told her that Allen was dead?

Allen was alive—alive, and he never came back for her!

Chapter Two

❧

Outside, she was grateful to take Dwayne's arm again and sense his strength as they strolled companionably along the avenue of quaint shops.

"Would you rather skip the show and just take a walk?" he asked quietly.

"Actually, I'm not feeling very well, Dwayne," she answered honestly. "I think I'd better go home."

She felt his disappointment as his hand wrapped around hers. Just ahead of them a commotion broke out. Several people ran out into the street, staring up in the sky.

Someone shouted, "Look, there's been a midair crash."

Maureen listened for the sound of falling metal. Was it a plane taking off from nearby John Wayne Airport? If so, run for cover! she thought. Don't just stand there.

But Dwayne Crocker was already propelling her toward the crowd. Overhead a brilliant, blazing light illuminated the sky. The resplendent glow of a rocket missile—dazzling, magnificent.

As if awakening a slumbering planet, the missile had split the heavens on soundless wings—mute, echoless as it soared into the clear evening sky. As she watched, it hovered to the left of Venus, shining brighter than the evening star. And then its diaphanous haze cut a course through the clouds, swirling into shimmering vapor trails, churning into eerie streamers.

Dwayne said, "That thing can be seen for a hundred miles."

She looked up at him. Crocker actually looked like some little kid whose kite had blown higher than his friend's.

"It just takes minutes to reach an island in the Pacific Ocean," she said. "Four thousand miles away, quick as a wink."

"That puts it at a missile range near the Marshall Islands."

She agreed. Now that he had pinpointed the location to the minute, she felt more inclined toward Dwayne than she had at dinner. In front of them, a young couple craned their necks looking up, a small child clutching their hands.

"What is it, Daddy?" the boy asked.

"It's a missile, son. Remember, we looked at a book about them the other night. And that's the planet Venus to the right," the father said, pointing toward it.

What was he? Six? Seven? At unexpected moments like this, Maureen felt a tightness in her chest, an ache that wouldn't go away, a fresh flood of shame that she had given her own child away. She looked at the father and volunteered, "That splendor in the sky is a first-stage separation from the missile. Those blue and orange colors in the sky are vapors that occurred right after the missile was launched and separated."

As she noticed the boy's interest wane, she told him, "It's like painting pictures in the sky."

"So that's what they did. Daddy, they spilt their paints."

Maureen's heart did flip-flops, as it often did when she thought of her daughter. To the boy's father she said, "What we're seeing with our naked eyes is nothing more than burned fuel and water droplets hitting the atmosphere."

Dwayne rubbed his jaw reflectively. Give it to Dwayne from a mathematical perspective and he would know to the nth degree how much water, how much fuel.

The vapor trails twirled and arced out of control as they moved from the center and spread across the sky. Maureen gripped Dwayne's arm to steady herself. Something was wrong! How had she stood here for two minutes without realizing what was happening? She hadn't made the connection. But she did so now. The Fabian missile had misfired.

"Dwayne, that was one of the Fabian missiles. Look at the way it blew apart—at the lights streaming across the sky, like they're exploding from the center. Out of control."

"Can't be, Maureen. The air force agreed to hold off testing any more of the Fabians until the flaws were ironed out."

But as another burst of streamers spewed from the center, he said, "You may be right."

Of course, I'm right, she thought. And if that was a Fabian launch, I'm in trouble. The misfiring of another missile would set the wires sizzling between her office and the Pentagon. She whispered, "I have to get back to the office."

"Let me go back with you."

"No." She was adamant.

As vice-president of Research Operations, her department was responsible for what was happening. And if Eddie McCormick was going to have her head, she didn't want Dwayne Crocker there to witness it. She turned abruptly and eased her way through the throng, walking hurriedly to her sleek sports car parked beside Dwayne's. She climbed into her car, the wheels squealing as she raced from the parking lot.

Twenty minutes later, she sat at her desk and dialed the Wallingdale Air Force Base. When she couldn't get beyond the duty officer, she slammed down the phone and called her friend at the Pentagon. As the phone rang, she glanced out into the evening sky. The lights from the missile had vanished completely. As suddenly as the brightness had erupted into the heavens, it had died away and floated into nothingness, leaving only the evening star surrounded by its unbroken layers of clouds.

Someone on the other end picked up the phone. "Roland Spencer," he said.

"I was hoping I'd catch you. It's Maureen Davenport, in California. Roland, they launched that Fabian missile ahead of schedule. What went wrong?" she demanded. "They promised to postpone the launch until we could work out the flaws—"

"I'm sorry. There was a mix-up."

"Not mine," she said tartly.

"Ours," he acknowledged grudgingly. "Look, sweetheart, I'm still your friend. Remember?" He had been her friend since her first visit to the Pentagon. "If I didn't have a flat top, I'd be pulling out my hair. So I'm tugging at my mustache instead."

"Not funny," she said. "McCormick is going to

blame me for not getting word to Wallingdale Air Base in time."

"They knew in time. I'll vouch for you. So stay calm. I just had a call from the commanding officer at Wallingdale Air Base. He apologized."

"Apologized? Half of southern California saw their blunder."

Spencer laughed good-naturedly. He had a throaty chuckle that always made his rimless glasses bob; she pictured them doing so. "The C.O. from Wallingdale said it was a splendid show that could be seen for a hundred-mile radius."

"So when does Larhaven get wind of it, Roland?"

"Whenever McCormick sends them an e-mail. Hold just a minute. I have a call waiting."

While she waited, she tried to picture Roland's square face and wide brow bathed in scowls. He was a solidly built man of forty-eight, twenty pounds heavier than he should be, and yet he cut a favorable impression in his army uniform with the rows of service ribbons across his broad chest.

He was back now. "It wasn't your mistake, Maureen. Larhaven wanted that missile to go off."

"But we had orders from them to delay it."

"That was Eddie McCormick on the line. He said for you to stay at the plant. He'll see you there in an hour. He has one of the Kladis brothers with him."

"Allen Kladis?"

"That wasn't the name. Would it make a difference?"

All the difference in the world, she thought.

"Allen is a reasonable man, Maureen. Much fairer than his father. We've met over some government contracts. Hope this misfiring isn't his kind of reverse reasoning. The Kladis brothers are determined to beat out the competition and merge with Fabian."

The kind of reasoning that Allen Kladis was capable of? she wondered. But Spencer called him "fair." That would be the Allen that she remembered. "Will the merger go through?" she asked.

"It looks like the boys at the Pentagon want another corporate giant. The White House agrees." He cleared his throat. "The merger will help maintain our position on the world market."

"But it all boils down to money?" That didn't sound like Allen. Or had he changed once he joined the family business?

"We'll put a ban on firing any more missiles until this thing gets settled, Maureen. I'll check things out on this end in the morning and get back to you. By the way, you're staying with Larhaven when they merge, aren't you?"

"If they want me." If *Allen* wants me, she corrected silently.

"Their loss if they don't. And if they don't, we'll find you a spot here at the Pentagon."

As she cradled the receiver, she unlocked the top desk drawer and slid out the oriental jewelry chest that Allen Kladis had given her when she was seventeen. She kept the chest at the office because, with all the security there, she felt it was safer than keeping it at home. And still accessible to her most any time she wanted to journey back to the past. She dusted it off with the back of her hand and then took a tiny key from her purse and unlocked it. As she swung the lid back, tears burned behind her eyes.

She spread the items out and lifted the velvet case

with the five-carat diamond from Carl. Then, unfolding a packet covered in tissue paper, she wrapped her fingers around the pink-beaded baby bracelet. Baby Birkland, it read. Maureen Birkland's baby. It was all she had of her infant daughter. The couple who adopted her baby took everything else. Her daughter. Her life. Her dreams.

Ten yellowed one-thousand-dollar bills were held together with a rusty clip, still unspent after almost twenty years. Maureen shrank back from the money even now, still seeing it as Alexander Kladis's payoff to a frightened seventeen-year-old, his silent warning to stay away from his son, to never use his son's name. A son who was still alive—not dead as Alexander Kladis had told her.

As she waited for Eddie McCormick to arrive, she picked up Allen's last note to her. Inside was the snapshot of himself, taken on board his carrier as it lay anchored near Cyprus. Her tears splashed on the picture— Allen at nineteen in his navy uniform, his sailor's hat perched cockily on his head, his enormous dark eyes smiling out at her.

She clutched the snapshot and took up his note. She could almost hear him saying,

Dear Reeny,
I see you always in our last happy moments together. Mostly at the winter campsite where you sat on the log beside me above that frozen brook and wrote so intently on your notepad, I love you. I look forward to the day when I will see you again, Reeny. I am counting the days until this winter of separation is gone and we are together always.

Last, Maureen unfolded the letter that she had written as a seventeen-year-old. Words written to Allen, about Allen. Words that she had never sent to him.

Dear Allen,

I love getting your letters, but I wonder if I have them all. Sometimes Mother beats me to the mailbox. But would she keep your letters from me?

I have learned to listen for the mailman's truck on the street behind ours and to hurry outside and wait for him to reach our block. When I do that, he waves and gives me the mail. Allen, I tuck your letters inside my pocket so Mother will not see them. And at midnight, when everyone is sleeping, I read them.

Mother tells me we are too young to be in love. It makes me sad. I want my mother to like you. To be nice to you. We were such good friends and now she seems like a stranger to me. My loving you has hurt her. She kept asking me about that weekend we went away together. Five months ago now. She knows.

Two weeks ago she took me to the doctor. Mother is furious with us. And so I must tell you that I am carrying your child. I am five months pregnant. Yes, I am going to have a baby. Your baby, Allen.

At first I was terrified. I didn't know where to turn. I couldn't tell anyone, not even my friends at school. I tried to hide it from Mother as long as I could. When we left the doctor's office, she wouldn't speak to me. Even now I can hear Mother upstairs, packing what we will take with us. She insists that we must move. She will not allow me to disgrace the family name.

I have refused to go back to Indiana with her. And so we are moving to Running Springs. But I will not be far away. I have promised you that I will wait for you. No matter what Mother says, I will be here.

Your father came to our house again last week. But Mother would not let me see him, not the way I look now. But I was leaning over the banister and heard her tell him to go away—the way she told you to go away. Your father insists that I must never see you again. Our parents are determined to keep us apart. But, dear Allen, summer is coming.

Of all the seasons, Allen, summer is best. For you will come again in summer. Back to me as you promised. For now, I feel like we have been torn apart like the dull brown leaves outside my window, drifting from the trees into the yard. Falling before their time.

Last month I found Cyprus on the map. I wish that I could be with you, but I am not as pretty as when you went away. I put my hand on my belly and it is full and round, blossoming with our baby. I am frightened, but I am glad, too, because it is part of you. I cannot touch your face or lips or hold your hands. If I could, I would put your hand on my belly and let you feel our baby kick.

Mother won't talk about her grandchild. She keeps me isolated at home, but when we move to Running Springs, I can walk in the woods over the red-soiled trails covered with twigs that do not snap and leaves that do not crunch. I will look for footprints not my own. I will be looking for your footprints, Allen, and pretending that you are there with me.

* * *

Maureen sat at her desk at Fabian Industries, crying. She had never mailed the letter. Twenty years ago, while she was still penning the words to Allen, the phone had rung.

"It's for you," her mother had called up the stairs. "Mr. Kladis is on the line."

"Allen? Is it Allen?"

"It's about him." Her mother's voice had sounded shocked, stricken. And as she handed Maureen the phone, she had said gently, "Darling, you must be brave. It's Allen's father."

Across the bottom of the letter, she had written the postscript that Allen would never read:

They tell me that you are gone now, Allen. Dead. Killed in Cyprus. Drowned in the waters near the island you loved. Your mother's island. Your mother's people.

I clamp my ears, not willing to hear those words. Surely they are lying to me—my mother and your father. How can you be gone and never know about the baby? You promised to come back to me. And I sit alone, feeling our baby kicking inside of me. Our baby is alive, and you are dead. I am so afraid. And I weep because you will never know about our child. No. They are lying to me, dear Allen. I must keep listening for your footsteps, longing for summer to come.

Maureen heard Eddie McCormick's thudding, dragging steps coming down the corridor, then his voice speaking heatedly to someone else. The footsteps stopped, doors from hers, the argument between the two men raging. Maureen placed her treasures back into the jewelry strongbox, the beaded baby bracelet on top of Allen's picture, her unmailed letter folded beneath them.

She shut out the sound of the men in the corridor. Allen is alive, she thought. And Allen was married to someone else. Like I was married to someone else so briefly. The seasons had closed in on both of them. Still, she felt sadness for him. Allen with his unforgettable smile was too young to be a widower already.

Chapter Three

Maureen pulled herself forward, her arms resting on the desk, her hands clasped. Her eyes remained closed. Even when she opened them seconds later, it was as though she faced a thick fog bank, the white vapors slowly lifting, a figure coming to meet her. It was an image at first, swirling her back in time...and then a remembered face. A remembered time. A remembered place.

Allen—the memory of all her yesterdays, the unhealed wound of her quiet tomorrows. Allen—tousled and barefoot in a blue wet suit, a surfboard under one arm. Allen—defiantly facing her mother, declaring his undying love for Maureen. Allen in uniform, turning back to wave as he boarded the plane that would carry him back to his ship. The ship that would take him to Cyprus.

Allen! Allen, out of her life so long ago, yet crashing back into her thoughts again and again. Refusing to leave on this harried evening as she sat alone at Fabian Industries.

It had not been like that with Carl Davenport, the vigorous, fun-loving man she had married. There had been good moments with Carl, but when he died, her grief had been measured. She had grieved for Carl, a dignified sorrow for someone who had been special. She remembered him periodically with sadness for his fast-paced commitment to racing, to living, even to her. With sadness for the dynamic, energetic way he lived, the foolish way he died.

Whenever she thought of Carl, she recalled a laughing, spirited man who lacked nothing financially, and yet who sacrificed everything careening around a race course. Sometimes on holidays or special occasions, Maureen still visited Carl's mother in her isolated fifteen-room estate, enduring the long hours of a mother's reflections while the elderly woman talked as though her son would walk into the room any minute.

With Allen, it was different. She had no ties with Allen's family. The twenty-year-old memories were her own. She had grieved deeply for Allen, and when she remembered him now, she did so with searing intensity and always with thoughts of his child—a grown young woman now whose image she couldn't conjure up to comfort her. That part of Allen that she could only think of as "Meggy."

Allen. The well-remembered face of her first love with its Athenian features, a lock of wet black hair cresting over his broad forehead, the mesmerizing dark-brown eyes, the amused tilt of his head as he waved goodbye. A remembered time: high noon on the hard-packed beach. The sliver of a midnight moon peeking through the trees. The five o'clock flight that left on time. And the remembered places: Huntington Beach Pier, the isolated campsite at Big Bear, the crowded terminal at John Wayne.

Now with missiles and mergers and mayhem crowding in on her, it could well be Allen Kladis who would unknowingly take her down, topple her corporate climb— A sharp knock on her door announced Eddie McCormick's arrival. Without waiting for Maureen's reply, McCormick shoved open the door and came in, a dark-haired stranger behind him.

She caught her breath. It was like seeing Allen walk into her room, the stranger's likeness to Allen was so striking. Her palms dampened; her locked fingers tightened. She looked away, her eyes focusing on Eddie McCormick.

"Davenport, what in blazes went wrong this evening?" McCormick roared.

She steeled herself for a dressing-down and prepared to fight back, but at the sight of Eddie's ashen face, she bit her tongue. The once robust man came across the room in a halting gait, strands of his sparse gray hair falling limply across his forehead. A year ago he'd been a giant of a man, but his illness was taking its toll.

"Well, Davenport, do you have an explanation for what happened tonight with that missile?"

"Eddie, I didn't give that order."

"Who then? Some idiot in your de-department."

She heard the quiver in his voice, knew that his anxiety was peaking. She considered offering him a chair, but thought better of it. These days he took common courtesy as unwanted sympathy. She did pity him, but not in the usual sense of the word. She ached for him. She hated his struggle for control, his need to blame.

Lately he had taken to standing with his hands folded, his stronger one gripping his left wrist in a futile attempt to control the tremors. Tonight he stood with his left hand in his pocket, but she could still see the jerking of his upper arm.

Parkinson's disease is a cruel adversary, she thought.

She was accustomed to discussing industry problems with Eddie, but the thought of Allen Kladis's brother standing in the shadows, listening to her, was disconcerting. She tried to keep a clear head, saying, "The order to launch was phoned in to the air base, but no one in my department gave that order, Eddie."

"A gremlin?" he scoffed.

She ignored his sarcasm. "I talked with Roland Spencer at the Pentagon. He insists that someone at Larhaven made that call."

McCormick dropped in the chair across from her. "I didn't want the Pentagon involved."

"Our contract is with the Pentagon. You are familiar with the last communication from them. No more tests on the Fabian missiles until the problems are corrected. I had nothing to gain by giving an order to the contrary."

"My position," McCormick said. "You'd like that, wouldn't you? Taking over before Larhaven does?"

She didn't argue. That had been the original plan. He would take an early retirement, and Maureen, groomed and qualified to fill the job, would have been Fabian's first female CEO. Her disappointment at missing that opportunity was as keen and sharp as his mood swings.

Moving to the top had slipped through her fingers. Once Allen Kladis learned that she was on the corporate rung at Fabian, what chance did she have? Allen had always liked competition—but from his first love? If he had wanted to see her again, he would have come back long ago, wouldn't he?

Sighing, she said, "Eddie, what matters now is who

gave that order at Larhaven. And whether it will affect our government contracts." She aimed her barb at the stranger. "As far as I'm concerned, Eddie, we're still in business until Fabian and Larhaven sign on the dotted line."

"Seems to me it is a bit more involved than signatures," the stranger said.

Maureen allowed herself to look at him again, forced herself to do so. She drew in another quick breath. He was a shorter, heavier version of Allen, and equally attractive if it weren't for the cunning twist of his mouth. In that flash she likened him to his father. She had seen the head of the clan twice—a stocky, powerful man, a tad over five-eleven, with an authoritative voice and steely black eyes. His wide mouth had curled at the corner—exactly the way this man's was doing now.

She wanted to cry out, to ask about Allen.

The stranger eyed her curiously. He was casually dressed in dark slacks, an open-neck shirt, a forest-green sports jacket. He held up his hands and shrugged. "I'm a Kladis, but I don't give the orders." His voice was deep, half-amused, and his eyes mocking as they met hers. "That's my brother's department."

Even without the name, she would have guessed it. The family resemblance was definite, the voice quality so much alike. "Allen Kladis?" she asked, thrusting the name between them, challenging him, hoping that he would speak of his brother.

"I'm Nick. Allen's my elder brother, the company CEO."

"The owner of the company, then? The one who would have given the order to the air base. Call him. Find out what's going on."

He winced, his gaze shifting quickly to McCormick

and then to a space beyond Maureen's desk. "Mr. Mc-Cormick, you told me you'd get to the bottom of this."

He nodded. "But, Mr. Kladis, this is Maureen's department."

Nick turned his gaze on her again. "Then I think you're making a mistake, Miss Davenport. Larhaven had nothing to do with that launch."

"*Mrs.* Davenport," she corrected. "And Roland Spencer rarely gets it wrong." She had to hear Allen's voice—to know that he was really alive. "Why don't you call Mr. Kladis and find out what's going on?"

His eyes and tongue snapped at the same moment. "You're out of line, Davenport. We wouldn't do anything to stop the merger."

Wouldn't you? she thought.

She knew that she wanted to place the blame for the misfired missile on Allen Kladis. But even more, she wanted to hear his voice.

"The number?" she said, lifting the receiver.

"Look, don't bother my brother now. Allen won't thank us for calling him this late at night."

"Then when? When *can* I discuss this problem with him? The reputation of Fabian Industries is at stake," she said evenly. "I have to have answers when Roland Spencer calls in the morning."

"That's why I'm here. I'm capable of making company decisions." He glanced at McCormick.

But Eddie seemed at a loss for words. She wanted to cover for him. "We should stop production on the Fabian missiles," she suggested. "Can I tell Spencer you've given the order for that?"

He nodded. "If that's what you think best."

"You'll lose the government contract that way," Nick argued.

"It will just affect part of the assembly line. The tests for the flaws will go on. It's a good program. I dare say your brother will be pleased for the millions it will bring in."

"Finances? That's my department," Nick told her proudly.

She frowned. "I thought your brother Allen was CEO."

"Our father left the company to the three Kladis boys."

But he left Allen in charge, she thought. She was certain of that. He had been grooming his eldest son for the job. It had been the reason that the elder Kladis didn't want Maureen standing in the way.

"Oh, Allen got his hog's share of the company all right. Fifty percent. But Christophorous and I are still in the running."

She heard the bitterness in his voice.

"Christophorous?" she asked.

"Chris, the kid brother. The one who likes flying better than building planes. Couldn't care less who runs the company."

For some reason she remembered Allen calling him the "waif" of the family—the non-Greek, the question mark, the independent thinker. "Dad will never mold him. He came along ten years after the rest of us. Blond and fair-skinned and Mother's favorite."

But it was Allen who mattered to Maureen.

She stood silently, the receiver dangling between her fingers. Staring straight into Nick Kladis's dark gaze she asked, "Did you give that order to launch the missile, Mr. Kladis? To help the merger go through quickly?"

He didn't answer, but Maureen was certain that she

had struck a bull's-eye. If Nick gave the order, was Allen even aware of it?

"Were you trying to humiliate Fabian Industries? Trying to force the bidding figure down?"

Or were you trying to undermine Allen's leadership? she wondered. She had to talk to Allen. Or had Allen changed? Had he become shrewd and cunning like his brother Nick? As cagey and cruel as his father had been?

"I need answers, Mr. Kladis."

"Wait until I tell my brother that a woman is handling the missile project." He laughed sardonically, his dark eyes smiling nonetheless.

He was outwitting her for now. "Will you be around in the morning?" she asked.

He made a point of pushing back his cuff, glancing at his expensive watch. "It's already morning. I'll be flying out in a few hours. But we can talk by phone when you know what happened."

You're behind it, she thought. But why? You had no reason to destroy me, to tamper with my authority. But you're in a power play with your brother.

"Then we'll talk later," she said.

"I'll let Allen know." Again his eyes were mocking, amused.

Long after the men had gone, Maureen lingered at her desk, thinking about Allen. She had long ago come to terms with him dying on Cyprus, but to learn now that he was alive—that she had been deceived by both father and son—was unthinkable. Now the only picture she could conjure up in her mind was the youthful Allen, the young man she had fallen in love with, untainted by the Kladis's greed and conniving. But the businessman? The head of an aircraft company? Had he changed?

Meeting him again would be painful. Not meeting him would be unbearable.

Slowly she brought her attention back to the crisis at hand and jotted down notes for the morning schedule. At 2:00 a.m. she left a message on Dwayne Crocker's answering machine, asking him to meet her at eight in the morning. She had a vague recollection of him talking about new statistics that would iron out the flaws on the Fabian missile project. She wished she had listened more closely. It was the most important thing he had said all evening.

When she came face-to-face with Allen Kladis, she wanted answers that would guarantee her own job, and secure her reputation. Dwayne Crocker, with his mathematical genius, could give her those answers.

She tidied up her desk, closed up her office and locked it, then went through the security checks with a forced smile and a pleasant good-night to the security guards as she walked out to the parking lot. The night was mostly gone, but automatically, as she reached the car, she glanced up and saw the evening star still glowing brightly in the pre-dawn sky.

Chapter Four

In the Pacific Northwest, on what proved a surprisingly warm and dry spring morning, Allen Kladis moved barefoot across the thick carpet of his condominium. He paused at the mantelpiece, staring down at Adrian in the framed picture of their wedding day. Setting his water tumbler down, he braced his hands against the shelf, his gaze fixed on the bride and groom in the photo. His chest constricted, the emotional pain tormenting him with its harshness, its swift onset. It was a pain that never completely went away.

Had they really been that young, that jubilant? He saw it now, their absolute trust as they looked at each other, so confident that they had a lifetime ahead of them, not just twelve years. He felt cheated, robbed too soon of his dearest friend.

Adrian at twenty-three had been beautiful in satin and lace, his grandmother's clutch pearls around her slender neck. In the photo, she had just tilted her chin up, her blue eyes meeting his. Brilliant peacock-blue eyes. She looked so trusting, sheltered there in the crook of his arm. He looked rather striking himself in his black tuxedo.

"A handsome pair," the photographer had said.

Allen slid his tumbler across the fireplace shelf and moved three steps to the other picture of Adrian by herself. He had taken it two days after meeting her out by Snoqualmie Falls, where the 268-foot waterfalls had drenched them. In the photo she was laughing, pushing her wet, windblown hair back from her lovely face.

Without these two photos and without the shoe boxes of snapshots that she had hidden under the bed—photos she was always going to put in albums when she found the time—Allen would not remember how beautiful she had once been.

Adrian at thirty-five had been barely recognizable. Holding up his tumbler of iced water, he saluted her. "I still miss you," he said.

A year and a half ago she had been the healthiest woman he knew. Then, within weeks, she was suddenly tired, not feeling well, nauseated. Oh, Adrian, he thought, forgive me. I was so elated, so certain you were finally embarking on a rolling sea of morning sickness. A baby. The baby we always wanted. But you knew, didn't you?

He tilted his head back and ran one hand through his thick hair, still wet and unruly from the shower. He tried to block out the memory of picking her up in his arms that day and saying, "If you're pregnant, you'll make me the happiest man on earth."

Her smile had matched the glow in the photograph. But ten seconds after twirling her around and setting her down, she ran to the washbasin, deathly pale, deathly sick. When they saw the family doctor the next morning,

Allen grinned and said, "Just tell us, Doc. When is the baby due?"

Allen had never considered any other diagnosis until the doctor came back into the examining room. "Adrian is not pregnant," he said kindly. "But let's run some blood tests and see what's making her so tired. I'll call you when the reports come back."

Four days later he referred them to a hematologist. "What's wrong?" Allen asked.

"Mr. Kladis, let's not get alarmed. Let's just see what the specialist says."

What he had said was "acute myeloblastic leukemia."

"What are you telling us?" Allen demanded, sitting with Adrian across from the large mahogany desk.

Calmly, the physician repeated the words and added his medical mumbo jumbo. "We'll do a bone-marrow aspiration and chemotherapy to induce remission. Chemo may give her an extra few months."

Allen had doubled his fist and lunged forward. If it had not been for the grace of God and Adrian's swift grip on his wrist, he would have knuckled the hematologist's jaw and silenced his bluntness.

"My wife is not dying!" Allen had shouted, his angry words bombarding the four walls. "She's as healthy as I am. We swim every day at the club. Sail on Lake Washington. Ski all winter. Don't come in here with your crazy diagnosis, doctor. My wife is pregnant. Take another look at those tests."

"Don't, Allen," Adrian had said, reaching across the chair and clutching his arm. "I'll be all right. You'll see. We'll fight this together."

But it was a crushing, one-sided battle. Five months later, he sat by her hospital bedside, barely touching her bruised hand, not holding her the way he wanted to do because her pain was too severe. She was shockingly thin. Dark half-moons clung beneath her sunken eyes. She had fought a good fight—but she was losing. For days she slipped in and out of consciousness. On that last day, she came out of the murky depths of a coma and cried, "Allen, take me home."

His grip tightened on the mantel as he remembered the lie fitly spoken. "I will, honey, as soon as you're better."

You knew I was lying, he recalled. But I wanted to take you home again.

A tiny smile had touched her cracked lips. "What's happening to me? Where do I go after this?"

"Honey, I don't understand. What are you asking me?"

"I'm dying. You know that, don't you, Allen?"

He nodded, not wanting to lie to her anymore.

Her chest heaved. "But what happens to me when I die?"

He'd spent hours thinking about that—a mahogany casket with a white-satin lining. A cemetery plot, six feet deep. A miserable memorial with useless platitudes. He didn't need anyone to remind him how lovely she was, how much he loved her. But Adrian hadn't wanted to hear about a casket or cemetery plot any more than he did. *She's talking about herself,* he thought. *About what happens to her when she dies.*

He had struggled to his feet, leaned down and kissed her lips gently, the weight and pressure of his chest forcing the oxygen tube to hiss. "Honey, I'll get the chaplain for you."

"No, don't leave me… I'm afraid. *You* tell me."

How *could* he? He didn't know. She winced as he took her hands. "You'll go to heaven."

"What's heaven like, Allen?" She closed her eyes, her breathing raspy. Then she was back again, fighting to stay alive long enough to find her answers.

He groped for lessons from his childhood: the memory of his grandmother talking about heaven. "It's a pretty place," he said. "I know that. Streets of gold. A river of life."

It kept coming back, thoughts he had ignored for years, and doubted for some of them. He saw desperation in her eyes and longed to comfort her. "There's no pain there, Adrian. No tears."

"How do you know?" Her words were barely a whisper.

"My grandmother. She believed all of that."

"No tears?" With great effort she lifted her hand and touched his bristled chin. "Won't I cry for you, Allen?"

He held her hand against his lips. "Not half as much as I will cry for you."

As he stood in his living room, his hand shook visibly as he put the tumbler down again. He gripped the shelf as he thought of Adrian asking, "Will those I love be there?"

"My grandmother is there."

"No one else?"

He nodded, tears coursing down his cheeks. "God," he had said. "God will be there. And his Son." His grandmother had said the Son would be on the right hand of the Father—that He would be there to greet His children.

The oxygen had bubbled as Adrian gasped for air, her breathing so labored that Allen held his own breath. "Don't leave me," he begged. "I love you."

Slowly she focused on him, her eyes more glazed now. "How do I get to heaven, Allen?" she whispered.

On the wings of angels, his grandmother had said. But he wasn't certain. He didn't know where truth ended and his grandmother had improvised on her picture of eternity. But he did remember Grams declaring, "The way to heaven is through Jesus."

He leaned down, his face on the pillow beside Adrian. "Jesus is the way. You won't go alone. Jesus is here to go with you." He was quoting his grandmother again, and saw a flicker of hope in Adrian's glazed eyes. "Jesus," he repeated.

"Jesus," she said. She pushed the oxygen prongs aside. "Hold me, Allen," she had cried.

And he did, tenderly, lovingly, gently caressing her, his cheek pressed against her own. Ten minutes later the nurse gripped Allen's shoulder. "It's over, Mr. Kladis. Your wife is gone."

He stared now at Adrian's photo on the mantel. "She's gone, Mr. Kladis," he repeated solemnly.

To heaven? Yes, he was certain Adrian had been borne on the wings of angels—surely his grandmother had told the truth—and that she was safely there now. Pain free. With not even a tear for him. But in the eleven months since her death, he had shed enough tears for both of them, buckets of them in the shower, more as he lay in the empty bed alone, crushing her pillow against his chest.

After her death, work became his salvation. He poured himself into the planned merger between Larhaven and Fabian. During Adrian's illness, the merger had been tabled. Now, with the threat of a third party bidding for Fabian, Allen had attacked the project with renewed energy.

He ran his hand over his bare chest, willing the tightness to go away. Unraveling to his height of six-foot-two, he secured the strings on his jogging pants and walked back through the house. He stopped to fill his tumbler with an iced soft drink before reaching the bedroom. The king-size bed remained unmade, the spread sprawled on the floor, his pillow pounded to shreds. He had turned out to be a poor housekeeper these last eleven months, depending instead on the woman who came in three days a week.

He grabbed the merger file from the dresser, opened the sliding glass door, and stepped out onto his veranda that overlooked Lake Washington. Sinking into the chaise lounge, he stretched out his lanky legs and propped his feet on the iron railing. Business magazines were strewn on the porch. He felt useless, weary at thirty-nine, empty inside. With a sigh, he carelessly dropped the merger file on the floor.

Even from where he sat, an eddy—a violent little whirlpool—swirled, spinning out of sync with the rest of the lake. It was headed nowhere, with nothing but dark churning depths beneath it. His life had been on replay all day, one scene after the other, hitting him full force and then dropping into the bitter pools of memory. It hadn't been this intense lately, but he guessed the upcoming anniversary of Adrian's death had much to do with his mood.

He heard his brother's footsteps coming through the veranda door. "Figured you'd be here. I just let myself in," Nick said.

Nick slid a porch chair over beside Allen and dropped into it. "Thought you had company, big brother. Guess you were just talking to yourself."

"When did you get back, Niko?"

"On the morning flight. Nonstop straight from

L.A.—haven't even checked in with the wife and kids yet."

"You never make them top priority. You did travel alone?"

"Scout's honor. Strictly business."

"Did Fabian give an excuse for the misfired missile?" Allen saw his brother's crafty eyes shift. "You didn't step out of line, did you, Nick? The agreement with Fabian was to wait."

"What's done is done. McCormick blamed it on one of his vice-presidents. And Davenport swears the air force blew it." He met Allen's gaze for a second. "Allen, one of the first things you better do when the merger goes through is get rid of Davenport."

"What's wrong with him?"

"What's wrong is he's a *woman.* Powerful, from what I gather. Her job should go, once we merge. Mark my words."

"That's my decision. McCormick we keep for a time. The next five names on their management team go. Straight off the top. That saves millions right off."

"Good. The top five snares Davenport. She won't like that."

"A personal problem, Niko?"

"We had a few words about the missile going off."

"Your problem. But if I find you had anything to do with firing that missile, Niko, you're on your way out, too. But don't worry, I'll give you a good retirement settlement."

Nick frowned. "I hate the way you play with my life. Allen, you have everything. Give me a chance."

"I've lost everything that was important to me."

"You're still running Larhaven Aircraft."

"Just keep that in mind. And, Nick, I've decided to

take that Wednesday meeting with the Board of Directors at Fabian."

"I tell you, Allen, I can handle it. Aren't you worried about clashing with Eddie McCormick?"

"No. He works with us or he bows out gracefully."

"Why don't you do the same, Allen? Take a leave of absence?"

"And put you in charge? You're not ready for the job."

Nick glanced morosely out on the lake. "I can handle it."

"Not the way I do."

Nick—dependable? Somehow he had always managed to slip into class as the bell rang, or to arrive at the table by the time their father finished his perfunctory prayer. But trust Nick to run the business or make major decisions? Not good.

"I'm going to see this merger through, Nick. Larhaven still has a good reputation. Let's keep it that way."

"What's that supposed to mean?"

"You don't take over until I'm dead. That's a promise I made to Mother. And with just three years between us, I'm apt to be around making decisions for a long time."

"We never know when our time will be up, Allen. Look at Adrian."

"We're not talking about my wife," he retorted.

For a few minutes silence hung between them like a dark cloud. Then Nick said, "Be glad you didn't have kids, Allen."

"I'd still have something of Adrian in my life then."

"It's not that Fran and I don't feel sorry for you—"

"I don't want your pity."

"That's why we haven't given it. I think my wife is

right. You can't go on mourning. Get out. Go on a date. Make yourself available." He tented his fingers. "Life goes on. Get on with your own."

"I suppose you have someone in mind?"

"What about one of the gals at Larhaven?"

Allen had already gone that route. He saw no need to tell Nick that he had dated twice since Adrian's death— both times a total fiasco, a botched evening, a wipeout. One was with his attorney's attractive new assistant. While dropping off a file he had asked for, she boldly suggested having dinner together that evening. The other foolhardy venture was with a divorcée living in the condo above his. They had been picking up their mail at the same time. In the midst of inconsequential chatter, the girl fessed up to an empty fridge and a growing hunger.

Through both dates, his wife's name seemed to worm its way into the conversation, and he knew that the evening was falling flat. All he could do was to pick up the tab—hefty on both occasions—and to offer his date a safe ride home. One elected to go alone by taxi, and his neighbor rode in silence back to their building.

No, it just wasn't the time yet to think seriously about a new relationship. He was still sorting out Adrian's loss, trying to adjust to an empty condo and the terrible ache in his chest that wouldn't go away. It wasn't that he would never marry again. To the contrary, he longed for companionship, needed it and knew deep down that he was not intended to live alone, that he was capable of another commitment. But not yet, not when he would still compare any other woman—no matter how lovely— to Adrian.

But he was ready to do battle with Nick because the subject had come up again. He didn't need the advice of his younger brothers about his social life or lack of one.

"No dating, Nick. Not yet."

"My wife has friends looking for an eligible bachelor."

"I'm not a bachelor. I'm a widower."

"You can't let this drag on forever. Adrian wouldn't want you to. With your mood swings, you'll mess up the merger."

"There was only one woman for me, Niko."

Nick cocked his head, a touch of mockery in his gaze. "What about that romance of yours back when you were wet behind the ears? The one Dad got all fired up about? Doesn't that count?"

This time the frown was Allen's. "Maureen?"

Maureen. The sun reflected off the lake, a gentle breeze blowing across the water carrying him back twenty years in time. He could see her face, her beauty, her youth. He could even remember the curve of her mouth, the cut of her chin, the softness of her skin. And those wide violet-blue eyes had blown him away. For just a flash he felt that same searing pain that he had experienced when he went on shore leave, back to her hometown to find her. She was gone. Gone without a trace.

"Her name—it was Maureen Birkland, wasn't it?" Nick asked.

"How did you know that?"

"Dad's old file on her. He never did like her, you know. But she was some looker. Dad had a picture of her in the file."

Allen nearly toppled out of the chaise lounge, but caught his balance, his feet straddling the chair. "What was Dad doing with a file on her?"

"You told him you were going to marry her."

I *was,* he thought.

"That marriage bit was a shocker, I'm here to tell you. You take off for a ten-day surfing trip to California, and the next thing Dad knows, you're not coming home. You're getting married."

"She was a sweet kid. What did Dad have against her?"

"He said she was a nobody, Allen. Poor family. No social standing. No money. No future. You know Dad. Only the best for his boys."

Allen hadn't seen it that way. They had met at a small café down by the beachfront. He was standing barefoot in the sand, his surfboard propped against the wall. He had just ordered a peach milk shake when he saw Maureen pushing her tawny hair back from her face and looking up at him with those magnificent eyes. He grabbed two straws and offered to share the shake with her.

She surprised him and accepted. They sat on the beach, side by side, as they drank the shake. Eighteen, not quite nineteen, he had toppled head-over-heels in love with her, his passions awakened in a way he had not understood. First love. And it had been real enough. She was working part time as a file clerk in a bank and going into her senior year of high school. Allen was bigtime. High school behind him, the job at his father's aircraft industry hooked.

"We'll get married," he had told her on their third date, "and move back to Seattle."

"Mother won't let me. I have to finish high school first."

Allen never hit it off with her mother. Mrs. Birkland had disliked him from the beginning. She knew his family was rich and didn't believe his intentions toward Maureen were honorable. She told Maureen he was using her—"a summer fling," she'd called it. But the more she opposed Allen, the more Maureen was drawn to him.

Nick's words thundered again. *A poor family. No social standing or money. No future.*

It hadn't mattered back then. He would stay in California and marry her. And his father had blown his lid. That's one reason I joined the navy, he thought. To break Dad's shackles, to guarantee my freedom. To find a way to support a wife.

"After you sailed to Cyprus, Dad flew to California to meet her. He figured anyone could be bought off. Must have worked."

Stunned, Allen sat there. Maureen Birkland had been his first girl that summer so long ago, his reason for not going back to work for his dad. And his dad had bought her off. No wonder she wasn't there when he went back to find her. After all these years, the realization still hurt.

Keep cool, he told himself. Don't let Nick goad you. If Maureen hadn't been bought off, Adrian would never have come into your life. With Maureen you had nothing but a few weeks. But at least with Adrian you had twelve happy years.

"Where is Dad's file on Maureen Birkland?" he asked.

"In storage. Can hardly think of Dad tossing anything away."

"I want it. Find it for me."

"Forget that old file. We have more important things to worry about. Your whole executive board thinks you'll blow this merger unless you snap out of this grieving process."

"Did you put that idea into their heads, Nick? You know I've been better lately. I'll take care of my private life. Leave the Larhaven-Fabian merger to me," he said acidly.

Nick had never learned when to back off. He sat there sullenly, twiddling his thumbs. "You've run the show for ten years ever since Dad's death, even though you never wanted the job. Let me have a crack at it now."

"Dad left the job to me because he knew I could handle it. You and Chris weren't ready for it."

"Chris doesn't want it. I do."

Nick was their father all over again. Greedy for power. Ready to cut down those who stood in his way. "Nick, I'm only going to say this once. I'm going to see this merger under way and running smoothly. Work with me or get out."

The wind had picked up. He felt as empty as the whirlpool spinning on the lake, as though his life were swirling out of control. It was tough having your family oppose you. Perhaps Nick was right. Maybe it was time to resign and let his brothers take over.

How he longed to escape to a cabin on the river, do nothing. How he longed for inner peace. Peace like Adrian had found. But he didn't know where to find it. And God, if He existed, seemed distant.

Chapter Five

❦

An hour down the Pacific Coast Highway from Maureen Davenport's apartment, a young woman with Allen's dark eyes and Maureen's smile and long thick lashes stood by the window of her parents' home, a bride's magazine clutched in her hand.

Outside, a violent windstorm was piping through the canyon, howling through the tree tops, and rattling the windowpanes where Heather Reynard stood. The gusting wind swept everything in its path, bending sign posts, crumpling tree limbs like tissue paper. A few logs slid down the hillside and were swallowed up in the yawning mouth of a ten-foot wave that surged along the rocky shoreline.

Still Heather and her family were lucky. Last week it had been the fires raging out of control in the Silverado Canyon, flames leaping and bounding and turning the sky from a brilliant red glow to a smoky-gray. It had destroyed homes in its path and turned them to ashes, leaving hillsides charred with an ominous black canopy that had made both people and animals homeless. A hundred acres had already burned. With the winds tonight, the hot spots of the recent fires in the Silverado Canyon and the San Bernardino foothills could flare up and fan into raging infernos.

Heather shivered, the chill of the windowpane cold against her arms. Not one twinkling star could be seen. The only movement was the light of a jumbo jet. A smoky haze lined the horizon, and rain clouds hid the Big Dipper. But as she crouched lower and stared out the window, she saw a full hazy moon lying low in the sky, peeking out from the clouds, round as a yellow pumpkin.

"Oh, Brett," she exclaimed, "come look at the full moon." Her fiancé crossed the room and slipped his arm around her slender shoulders.

"Beautiful," he said, but when she turned to face him, he was looking at her.

"Oh, Brett!"

"You said that already."

Brett Martin, at twenty-six, was a foot taller than Heather, and seven years older, his height and broad shoulders rendering him a fortress of strength that pleased her. He was as fair-skinned and blond as she was dark. His eyes were wide-set, his brows thick, his smile full. Brett was not handsome, but she thought of him that way. Her own good-looking knight, so wholesome with his brown maple-sugar eyes, eyes that made her melt when he looked at her, the way he was looking at her now.

"Brett, the storm is worse. I don't want you out in it."

"Honey, I have to drive back to Los Angeles this evening."

"Not in this wind. Mother's making up a room for you."

He sighed resignedly. "I have class at eight."

"And I want you alive so you can attend it. You can get up early. I'll even set my alarm and make you breakfast."

He looked doubtful. "Okay," she told him, "Mother can cook it for you. But I'm learning, Brett. By the time we marry, I'll be a pretty good cook. Mother is determined."

"With your unpredictable schedule with the airline, I hope she's successful. And if not," he teased, "I'll talk your mom into moving in with us."

"She wouldn't hear of it."

"Is she still opposed to our marrying in August?"

"No, she's resigned herself. She thinks I'm too young, but I'll still be too young when I'm thirty. Mothers are like that. And as long as I eventually finish college—"

The bride's magazine slipped from her fingers. Brett stooped to pick it up. "Then what's wrong, honey?"

"This miserable weather."

"We have no control over that." He lapsed into his lofty seminary voice. "The storms and winds come from God's storehouse. Oppose the weather and we oppose God."

"You're preaching again, Brett," she cautioned.

"That's what I'm training for, my darling."

"But you're not in the pulpit now, and I don't want you to sound that way ever. It's your openness and honesty that first attracted me to you, Brett. You're too genuine to play a role."

"Heather, all my life I've wanted to be a preacher. I'm a third-generation—"

"I want you to be what you want to be. But be yourself, Brett. Lost men and women are depending on you. They'll like you better and trust you more if you don't sound preachy."

"Do you have someone lost in mind?" he asked.

She nodded. "A woman I've never met."

"I'm not up to a guessing game. Who?"

"My birth mother. She may not know that God loves her."

"We just have to trust that she will," he said confidently.

Heather fell silent. Faith and simplicity were easy choices for Brett. He really did credit the winds and storms to God's storehouse. She leaned against him as his arm tightened around her.

"You look so upset, Heather. What's troubling you?"

"It's the guest list for our wedding. I want to invite someone and I'm afraid to tell you—and even more afraid to tell Mom and Dad."

He winked. "Let me guess. That older flight attendant who gives you such a bad time when you work together?"

"No, but we're doing much better now. Or maybe I'm doing better on the job."

"Not your old boyfriend? We agreed not to invite him."

"He's coming anyway. His family and mine are old friends."

"You want to invite someone you don't know to our wedding? Then you'd better tell me."

Her voice trembled. "I don't think you're going to like what I say—but I want my birth mother there."

The storm had moved inside. The way Brett looked down at her now, there was no way that his maple-sugar eyes could melt anything. He was obviously displeased with her decision.

"You can't be serious. What if she rejects you again?"

"That's cruel."

"She was cruel to leave you."

"But I won't know why she left unless I try to find her."

He turned to face her and placed his hands firmly on her shoulders. "You said your birth mother. What about your father?"

"Have you forgotten? He died before I was born."

"Do you know that for certain? Maybe he just ducked out. Some men are not willing to take responsibility."

"It's not like that, Brett. When I was adopted, Mom and Dad were told that he died in Cyprus on a peace-keeping mission."

"The army?"

"The navy, I think. I—" she faltered. "I don't really know. I used to ask questions, but I could see that it hurt Dad. Dad was afraid of losing me if I found my birth mother."

Brett looked more perturbed than Heather had ever seen him. His usually cheery face was taut with worry, perhaps even a touch of anger. "Heather, I thought we agreed that we would be honest with each other, that we would make major decisions together."

"I was afraid to tell you."

"So why is it so important now to find someone that—"

"That never cared about me?" Her voice cracked. "We don't know that. We don't know why she didn't want me."

He touched her cheek. "I don't want you to be hurt."

She groped for words. "Oh, Brett, you can't protect me from everything. There might be reasons why they gave me away. Reasons why you and I shouldn't have children."

"I'm willing to take the risk," he said. "You know that. We've talked about it. Seminary first. And then a family."

"And what if I get pregnant before you graduate? My birth mother was only seventeen."

"Seventeen? But you're almost twenty—and very mature."

"That didn't answer my question, Brett."

"If the babies come before I finish seminary—before you have a chance to finish college—then we'll welcome them. I can't imagine a greater joy than you being the mother of my children."

She was grateful to him. He was trying to stop the battle building between them, trying to protect her from the unknown. "That doesn't change anything. I still want to find my mother," she said again. "I *must* find her." She looked up and met his gaze. "I want to start our marriage with the record clean, with the questions about my birth parents answered. Whatever it takes, whatever the outcome, I want to find the woman who bore me. I want to know about the father I've never seen."

"But Nan and Todd—they've been good to you. They love you."

"I know that. They'll always be Mom and Dad. My parents. But there's a part of me that still feels a void inside."

He drew her into his arms. "I thought I made you happy."

She reached up on tiptoe and kissed him—a light,

feathery kiss. "You do. I love you. But I'd be so much more complete if I knew who I was."

"You're Heather Reynard. You're going to be Heather Martin. That's enough for me. Isn't it enough for you, honey?"

She shook her head. "Please help me find my mother."

He led her to the sofa and sat beside her, his head in his hands. "What if we haven't found her when August rolls around?"

Only the sounds of the storm filled the room. Outside the torrential rain washed away the sight of the moon from the sky. Lightning flashed across the horizon. Thunder roared in the distance. Rain splashed the windows, pelted the tiled roof, and ran in widening rivulets down the hillside.

"I asked you a question," he said gently. "Tell me."

"Does helping me depend on it, Brett?"

"No," he said huskily. "It's your life. Your past. I can live with things the way they are. I don't think you can."

"Neither do we," Todd Reynard said from the doorway.

"Oh, Daddy. I didn't mean for you to hear."

"And I didn't mean to eavesdrop. Your mother sent me down. She was worried that your young man here would be foolish enough to try driving home in this storm. She has his room ready."

Todd Reynard ran his hand nervously through his hair, causing a tuft of it to stand up wildly. He was a solidly built, pleasant-faced man of average height, with eyes that usually danced when he talked with Heather.

"What should I tell your mother?" he asked.

"He's staying, of course," Heather said.

As Todd turned to leave, Brett stopped him, saying, "We were talking about the guest list for the wedding, sir."

"Yes, Brett. I overheard," Todd said apologetically. "Don't let me disturb you."

"But this concerns you and your wife. I think the four of us should talk it over, sir." He glanced morosely at Heather. "What do you think, honey?"

Heather nodded. "I didn't mean to cause trouble."

"Then let's put everything on the table—out in the open." He glanced at Todd. "Why don't you call your wife down?"

They watched Heather's dad go to the foot of the stairs. "Nan, dear!" he called. "Could you come downstairs for a bit."

"Don't be ridiculous, Todd," came a lighthearted voice. "I'm in my nightclothes."

"It's all right. Just throw your robe on and come join us."

Minutes later she came into the room in her bathrobe, her feet bare. "Is something wrong?" she asked, her gaze going worriedly from face to face.

Todd pulled her down in the chair beside him and squeezed her hand. "The children have something to say."

They could hear her sigh above the pounding rain. She sat motionless, an expression of alarm frozen on her face. "The two of you—?" she faltered. "You're all right?"

"We're fine," Brett said. "But we need to talk to you about the guest list for the wedding."

Nan's voice filled with exasperation. "You called me down at this time of night for that? We have four months before the wedding. Honestly, Heather, dear, put the name on the list, get an address—'' She picked at the lint on her worn robe. "If there's a problem we'll talk about it in the morning."

"We don't have an address," Brett said.

"We don't even have a name," Heather added.

Nan's voice wavered now as she said, "I don't understand."

Todd ran both hands through his hair, his fleshy cheeks drained of color. "I think you do, Nan."

Nan looked at her husband and then away. "Oh, dear. I guess I expected this." She sighed and covered her mouth with her hand.

"Mom, if you and Daddy don't want me to—I'll just forget it. I wouldn't hurt you for anything in the world. It's just—"

Brett folded his hand over Heather's and gave it a reassuring squeeze.

"Are you certain, Heather, that this can't wait?" Nan asked tearfully. "Couldn't we take care of this after the wedding?"

"Finding missing persons takes a long time," Todd said, his eyes downcast.

Brett's hand tightened around Heather's. "Nan, Todd," he said, "I told Heather it doesn't matter as far as I'm concerned. That you are her mom and dad and that's good enough for me."

"But not for you, Heather?" Nan asked.

Brett cleared his throat. "I think Heather is willing to put off the wedding if she has to. It's that important to her."

They were talking in circles, all of them knowing what Heather wanted without saying the words. Heather lifted her face and felt the defiance and tears come at the same moment as she looked across at the parents who had raised her.

"I love you," she said. "Surely you must know that! You're the ones who adopted me—the Mom and Dad who loved me through the ups and downs of my rebel years. You prayed for me. Prayed for my future." She smiled up at Brett. "You prayed for the man I would marry. But there has always been a question mark about my beginnings."

Nan nodded. Before Todd could protest, she reached across and patted her husband's knee. "Yes, Heather, dear, we know that you love us…" Her voice trailed. "But, Heather…Brett, it's your guest list. We promise, we won't interfere."

"Mom. Dad," Heather whispered. "Then you don't mind if I search for her? Please help me. I want to find my birth mother before my wedding day. There's so much I want to know…so much I need to tell her."

Her father's smile turned ragged. "We love you, Heather."

Nan straightened her shoulders and said bravely, "But right now that isn't enough, Todd."

"Not enough?" he asked. "We've done—"

Nan reached across and touched his lips. "It has nothing to do with what we've done, Todd. We've seen this coming—"

"Please, Mom…Dad."

Her dad looked as lost as Heather felt as he glanced at his wife for confirmation. Then he cleared his throat as he turned back and faced her. "It's your decision. Your Mother and I will stand by you."

Outside, the rain kept coming down in torrents. The howling winds whipped up, pushing the rain against the patio door. Lightning streaked across the sky. Claps of thunder bolted and roared back. The electric lights in the room blinked, then blacked out, and they were left in total blackness—a darkness nearly as palpable and pervasive as the empty space in Heather's heart.

Chapter Six

As the jet rolled down the runway at SeaTac International on a nonstop flight to southern California, Allen Kladis shut out everything, even the presence of his brother Nick beside him. The last thirty-six hours had revitalized Allen. Once he decided to fly south, he was in charge again. Galvanized by Nick's mishandling of the merger and by the strong possibility of Nick's involvement in the missile launch, Allen took back the reins that had been slowly slipping from his grasp. Larhaven was his responsibility, the planned merger totally his own doing.

He was the old Allen—efficient and forceful, brisk and robust. With renewed energy, he set the wheels in motion, jumping on track like a car running on new spark plugs. Yesterday he had called an emergency meeting with his executive board. Assignments were delegated with definite nods of approval from the older men. Nick slid into his chair five minutes late, shock registering on his face when he saw Allen conducting the meeting.

It took Allen's secretary ten seconds to see what was happening—and she was off, gathering up the reports that he needed. Booking him a flight on the airline seemed to please her most.

Vangie had been with him for ten years so she said, "I'm glad you're going, Mr. Kladis. Your brother Nick—I don't like to say it, but he still needs your supervision."

At the last minute, Allen agreed to take Nick with him, and Vangie went off with a satisfied smile to book two reservations for Tuesday.

For the first time in eleven months, Allen had whistled as he showered and packed. He'd even made a last-minute call from the airport to his brother Chris. "Christophorous, is your invitation for a Canadian camping trip still on...? Good. I'll be back in time, raring to go."

He had stood there grinning like an idiot into the receiver. "That's right, little brother. I'm ready to go camping or even flying with you in that Cessna of yours..."

Another pause and then he added, "And, little brother, I'd like to talk to you about taking flying lessons. Yeah, me. I'm ready to soar."

So here he was, flying off on a business assignment for the first time in months, sitting in first-class with his attaché case stowed in the overhead above him and allowing his thoughts to shift to Adrian. His thoughts of her were pleasant ones, not memories draped in sadness. He found himself smiling, an unexpected sense of peace and freedom surging through him. It was like taking a quick glance at her picture on the mantel or her snapshot in his wallet. But somehow it was different this time. It was like checking in with her to see how he was doing. He knew she'd be pleased that the old Allen was back in charge. Right now, it was as though he wanted to flood his memory with her and then really let her go, to let her soar free from the bounds of earth and from his lingering hold on her. *Adrian.*

Promise me, she had said, *that you won't grieve. That you will let yourself love someone again.*

He had promised, never believing he would lose her. But Adrian had been borne on the wings of angels away from him. He could no longer bring her classic features clearly into focus. Still, these were good memories, as though he'd raked through the bitterness and was taking stock of his future.

Looking down on a ribbon of clouds, he had the feeling that they had both broken the bounds of earth. He had reached a pivotal point over these last few months, and knew that life was still worth living. He didn't have to hang on to the past or even know what the future held. Companionship, he hoped. Even the thought was guilt-free. He wasn't looking, but then he hadn't been looking when Adrian came into his life.

The challenge of working was back. He wanted Larhaven to continue as a top competitor in the aircraft industry. But, unlike his father, he wanted to retire early. He was wealthy enough to do so now, but he had to hang on until he was convinced that Nick could take over. Allen felt like a man at the top of a ski slope, ready to take the mountain. The change had crept up on him. But he felt alive, whole again. The ache inside was still there, but he knew there would be good days ahead.

He grabbed an envelope from his pocket and jotted down the things that he and Adrian had always planned to do: Paris in the spring, a night course on computers, and a crash course in German. Then he struck a line through each one. That was part of his past: Adrian's goals, no longer his own.

What do I want to do? he asked himself. I'm on my own now. And he wrote down several things: Retire in five years. Travel abroad. Take flying lessons—see Chris about this one. And then he wrote, *Pursue peace.*

He stared at the words. What had possessed him to write them? Adrian again? No, his Grecian grandmother. She was an old-fashioned woman with the old country ingrained in her life-style. She wore black mostly—shawls, dark stockings and laced-up shoes. But she was bubbly and full of pearly bits of wisdom. When she hugged you against her ample bosom, you felt secure.

"Allen," she had predicted, "when you have dollar bills coming out of your ears and you're stinking rich like your father, you won't be happy. My son never was." She had squeezed Allen's hand. "There's something more to life than making a good living. You find it, Allen. Then you can help Nick and Chris."

He lifted the pen to cross off the words, then changed his mind. What was wrong with pursuing peace? Allen looked out the aircraft window. The jet was beginning to rumble and bounce from the turbulence. The clouds beneath were gray-white, uneven like snowdrifts.

For the last fifteen minutes, Nick had wandered restlessly through the first-class cabin, talking to other passengers. Now he was up by the kitchen keeping his balance with his feet apart, a third cup of coffee in his hands. And flirting with another flight attendant. Nick pointed toward Allen and the attendant peered around the kitchenette.

Now, I can expect sympathy and pity that I don't want, Allen thought.

Allen leaned back in his leather seat and thought about

his brothers. Things were going better with Chris, but he was always at odds with Nick. Putting him down. Never thinking he measured up. But that was the way his father had treated all three of them. So he wrote on the back of the envelope: Reconcile with your brothers, particularly with Nick.

The seat belt sign flashed on. Nick would be back, talking nonstop all the way to John Wayne. Allen glanced ahead and saw Nick groping his way down the aisle. As Nick dropped in his seat and fastened the belt, he asked, "What are you doing, Allen?"

"Writing out my want list."

"That's kid stuff. My sons do that all the time. Christmas wish list. Birthday list. Any holiday they can throw in."

Allen thought, I should spend more time with Nick's kids. Start being the kind of uncle they need.

"Have you put down dating yet?" Nick asked.

And surprisingly, Allen laughed. "Did you have the flight attendant in mind?"

"I did, but she's already married."

"You're a lucky man, Niko. Do you realize you have a family at home who adores you?"

"Fran and five bickering sons? They're the reason I like getting away."

Allen had always liked his sister-in-law, and often wondered why Fran had ever married Nick. He tried to see things from Nick's perspective, but couldn't. "I don't understand you, Nick. But Adrian always said you'd come to your senses one day and realize what a gem Fran is. Fran has been like a rock to me this past year."

"You two seemed pretty chummy at the airport."

"She was taking me down a notch. Told me enough

time had gone by. It was time to clean up my act and clean out my condo.''

"You let Fran get by with that?''

"My place is a mess even with house help. Fran said when I get back all of Adrian's clothes will be gone. Her tennis racket. Her ski gear. Everything.'' He felt a tick pulsating along his jaw. "Nick, I'm glad Fran stepped in. I told her to take whatever she wanted, but she said she would leave no reminders anywhere.''

"She'll take care of them for you, Allen. She'll probably cart them off to the church down the block from us.''

"Does she go to church?'' Allen asked.

"Across town somewhere. She takes the kids. I don't go, of course. But Fran refuses to raise a bunch of heathen.''

Allen laughed. "If she's collecting heathen, maybe I'll go with her sometime. Would that be all right?''

"The kids would love it if Uncle Allen went with them.'' Nick faced his brother. "You're really beginning to let go, Allen.''

"I'm going to need your help, Nick.''

The look on Nick's face was one of shock...and then pleasure. "You need me? You're not putting me on? You always seem more interested in Chris.''

"Chris doesn't fudge on contracts or cut corners to make more money. He comes from a different mold, Nick. Maybe he is more like Mama.''

"But he's not satisfied just building planes. He has to fly them. The way he tinkers with the engines, I'm not sure executive row is the place for him. He should be on the assembly line.''

"I think you're right, Nick. Running the business—

hassling contracts—that's not Chris. Making planes fly—that's Chris.''

"Ladies and gentlemen," the pilot's voice interrupted their conversation, "we will be landing in Orange County in fifteen minutes. For your own safety…"

Allen stretched his lanky legs, working out the cramp in his right calf. He tucked the pillow behind his neck and glanced out the aircraft window as the plane banked and lowered for landing. As the plane descended into Orange County, they were in a race against sunset and darkness, the clouds overhead swirling and black. He had one pleasant thought as the jet screamed across the runway and braked and jolted to a complete stop at Gate Twelve. His grandmother had always said that life was full of surprises.

On Wednesday Maureen Davenport walked through the shiny glass doors of the hotel, hoping she looked polished and professional in her slim navy suit with its interwoven silver-and-pink threads. Gripping her faux alligator attaché case, she hoped to project the picture of success—not the shy, bashful teenage girl that Allen had first met.

Maureen's thick, tawny hair was cut short and brushed to a brilliant sheen. Her nails had been done an hour ago and her makeup carefully applied. At the last minute she switched from a dazzling gloss to a subdued pink lipstick. She was wearing pierced earrings and the same brand of French perfume that Allen had given her the day before he went away twenty years ago. She had even worn the sapphire silk blouse that brought out the violet-blue of her dark-lashed eyes.

You will be shocked when you see me, Allen, she thought. I am older, sophisticated, worldly wise. Not the gangly seventeen-year-old who fell in love with you. The girl you abandoned without a word of farewell. You are the father of my child, but you don't know that. So I will hold my head up when I walk into that conference room and look you square in the eye.

The glass door swung closed behind her. *What if Allen doesn't remember me? What if I* was *only a passing fancy back then…a momentary dalliance? A break from surfing the waves.*

Inside the lobby she felt unnerved, not prepared to face Allen at the conference table or anywhere else. But always the consummate businesswoman, she had come armed with reports and statistics. She thought that she was fully prepared for Allen's quick, clever comments or his persuasive ways. But was she?

She looked around for her colleagues and saw Eddie McCormick coming to meet her. "Why the hotel, Eddie?" she asked as he reached her. "Why aren't we meeting at the Fabian office?"

"A Larhaven decision."

Eddie McCormick's left hand shook slightly. Otherwise the onset of Parkinson's was not noticeable today. He still cut a good impression. He was appropriately attired in a business suit with a maroon striped tie, his thinning gray hair slicked down. His blue eyes looked faded, almost listless, as though age and illness had drained them of color and energy.

Maureen had resented it when he changed his mind about retiring. But now she was glad that he was the one to go head-to-head with Allen. "Are you going to fight for our jobs, Eddie?"

There was an imperceptible jerk of his head. "You're still wanting to buy that home of your own?"

"I've already put a down payment on it."

"Sitting high on the hill overlooking the ocean—is that a good idea, Maureen? I warned you. You're right in the path of canyon fires and the floods."

"And don't forget the landslides. But I've been a risk-taker all my life."

He shoved his hands in his pockets. "Everything is shaky these days."

She pitied him. McCormick no longer had the physical strength to head a company. He had been a good man until ill health caught up with him. But the truth was that she was more concerned about her own predicament. She wanted—no, needed—to keep her job. Without a steady job—without her present income—Maureen's dream home would be gone as surely as if it had been swept away in a mud slide and washed out into the Pacific.

"Eddie, you should have insisted on the location for this meeting. Why give in to the Kladis brothers before we have to?"

That wasn't fair, she knew. Coming to an agreement to merge had not been easy for Eddie.

"The hotel is neutral ground," he said. "Allen Kladis thought it best to meet here and not alarm anyone at Fabian."

"As though our employees are not sitting on the edge of their seats already. Everyone—and I mean everyone right on down to the mop boy and stock clerk—is expecting the worst."

"That's unreasonable. The merger is the salvation of Fabian. Our profits have dropped dramatically these last few years."

Seven men had joined them now: the vice-presidents and chairmen of different departments. Their greetings were reserved, Dwayne Crocker's wink more friendly.

Eddie led the way, the others falling into step behind him, and Maureen finding her strength by walking beside Crocker.

"You look great," Dwayne said, giving her a quick appraisal. "How about dinner tonight? We can start all over."

He grinned, so she smiled back. "I think not, Dwayne. I'm certain we'll be exhausted after this meeting with Larhaven."

She paused as she reached the conference room. Nick Kladis sat at the huge oval table, watching the men from Fabian file in. The man beside Nick sat at the head of the long table, his elbows propped up on the shiny mahogany surface, his square chin resting on his clasped hands.

Her heart pounded, her lips went suddenly dry.

It was Allen. He looked as striking as ever, his skin bronzed as though he were still surfing each day, the cut of his profile firm and strong, his dark hair combed back smoothly, his designer suit sharp and stylish.

"Go on in, Maureen," Dwayne said, looking puzzled. "Let's get this over with. If we still come out employed, I'll still stake you to a meal. You can choose the place."

"Some other time," she said.

"I'll hold you to it." He shrugged and stepped back, allowing her to go first through the open door.

As she entered the room, Allen Kladis looked up, a frown cutting between his brows. His marvelous rich brown eyes met hers, strayed, came back at once. He stared wide-eyed, his hands dropping away from his face. And Maureen knew that for Allen, there had been instant recognition.

Chapter Seven

Allen felt his neck grow warm as he sat at the head of the conference table. He couldn't bring himself to look at Maureen. As she took her seat, he ran his finger along the list of names on the notepad in front of him. He saw no Maureen Birkland. But he saw the name Mrs. Maureen Davenport, vice-president of Research Operations, with a string of degrees and special studies beside her name. *Mrs. Maureen Davenport.*

So she was married. Was that why she went away— why she had not waited for him to come back from Cyprus? But her mother had opposed marriage before her daughter finished high school, especially marriage to a nineteen-year-old surfer from Seattle.

"I will not give permission for Maureen to marry you," Mrs. Birkland had told him.

"Then I'll run away with him," Maureen threatened.

"And I will find you." The older woman stood defiantly, her face dark with anger. "Until you are eighteen, Maureen Birkland, you will do as I say. So get out of my house, Allen Kladis, and don't come back."

Fire had blazed in Maureen's magnificent violet-blue eyes. "Then, Mother, I'll marry Allen when I'm eighteen."

They ran off that weekend to a winter campsite up the mountain where they hiked in the woods along a frozen brook. He still remembered the snowflakes from the first snow clinging to Reeny's tawny hair. He had slipped his arm around her and told her, "I'm going away in six days, Reeny. I joined the navy."

She clung to him, crying, begging him not to leave her.

"I've already signed on the dotted line. I did it for us, Reeny. Once you're eighteen, we won't have to listen to our parents again. We'll get married."

"I won't be eighteen until July."

"But summer is coming," he had whispered in her ear. "We belong to each other—in our hearts, we're already married."

He had wanted all that went with marriage. Demanded it. He persuaded both of them that they didn't have to wait until July.

Nick nudged him. "Start this meeting, or I'm taking over. The Fabian team is nervous enough, waiting for the ax to fall."

Allen gave the team at the oval table a vague professional smile—friendly, but not too friendly. "Mr. McCormick, would you be so good as to introduce your people around."

Allen didn't hear the first three names. He nodded. Doodled on the paper in front of him. And then McCormick was introducing Maureen, running off a list of her achievements. But all that Allen heard or saw was her name and her lovely face.

The tilt of her chin warned him that there would be

no verbal recognition in front of her colleagues. Her blue eyes, as angry as they were as she looked at him now, still blew him away.

"Mrs. Birkland," he said.

"Mrs. Davenport," she corrected.

"Sorry." She had put him on the defensive. He fought back, saying, "Vice-president of Research Operations? That makes you the one in charge of the missile launchings at Wallingdale."

She shot an accusing glance at Allen's brother and said, "But not in charge of the misfiring of the last one."

Nick squirmed beside him. So what did that mean? What Allen had suspected: Nick had overstepped his authority.

The next three hours dragged on. First with Allen at the chalkboard. And then Nick. Maureen vetoed their proposals three times, challenging their validity.

She's a smart one now, Allen thought, the innocence and shyness of her youth no longer apparent.

There were some nods as Nick turned the flip sheets and unveiled the detailed charts that proved the Larhaven-Fabian merger would give them a strong footing in the global market.

Dwayne leaned forward. "Mr. Kladis, I see flaws in your numbers. A few revised calculations and we'll have it right."

Crocker was sure of himself. Bold, audacious. His challenge had been against Nick's charts, not Allen's authority; he respected Crocker's comments. Nick was a good man, but he could do with Crocker working beside him.

Allen felt a headache coming on, like a pelting rain against the windowpane—a steady, annoying beat. He had boasted of their place in the global market when they merged, and now he had to tell them about the layoffs. "McCormick will be staying on as CEO of Fabian, but some of the executive posts will be cut. I'll be bringing in my own management team from Seattle."

It's strictly business. Nothing personal, he told himself.

He glanced around the table, the sudden movement increasing the pain at the base of his skull. He reached up and massaged the back of his neck, feeling defeated, the same way he had felt the last time he faced Maureen's mother. *Get out, Allen Kladis, and don't come back.*

The door to the conference room was his escape. Or he could withdraw the Larhaven bid, and let the midwest company buy out Fabian. But that ran counter to Allen's competitive spirit. He knew that this was his golden egg, his chance to buy into success that would give him one of the top places in the world market.

He flipped open the folder and scanned the names of the Fabian team, their salaries and benefit totals beside them. The final column in red indicated the savings that would occur with each dismissal. He drew a line beneath McCormick's name and then counted off the next five officers. Maureen Davenport's name was among them. He was about to cut her to the ground.

He folded his hands and rubbed his thumbs together. "Those of you who will be asked to take an early retirement will be notified by certified mail. But let me assure you, you will be offered a substantial retirement package and three months' severance pay with health benefits for the first year."

Nick kicked him under the table. He took the warning and added, "Of course we will be more than willing to provide you with good references or discuss this with each of you privately.''

The whole miserable thing was coming out wrong. He'd spent three hours encouraging these people to believe that the merger was to everyone's advantage. Now he was telling them that several of them were expendable. His father had indulged in this type of cutback over the years and found peculiar satisfaction in stomping on other lives. Allen found the process more than distasteful.

Nick gave him another jab under the table, prompting Allen to say, ''Perhaps other positions will be available at the plant...if we could come to terms that match our budget.''

His gaze met Maureen's and held. Her chin still jutted forward. She had her mother's strength, and that remarkable determination that had almost destroyed him when Mrs. Birkland told him to go away. As he dismissed the meeting, she made a beeline for the door. He caught up with her in the hotel lobby.

''Maureen.'' She turned, unshed tears balancing on her long lashes, those velvet-blue eyes meeting his.

''Hello, Allen,'' she said, a catch in her voice.

''I never dreamed you were part of Fabian.''

''From what you said in there, I won't be for long.''

''Let me explain. Believe me, Maureen, the cutbacks were determined long before we flew down from Seattle.''

''That doesn't make it any easier.''

He saw her sudden movement as she turned to go, and felt suddenly like a schoolboy not wanting to let the Homecoming Queen get away. ''Can we have lunch together?''

''I'm not hungry.''

"I am. And I can't just let you walk away thinking—I don't know *what* you're thinking."

He struggled with his emotions: Adrian-Maureen, Maureen-Adrian. But Adrian was never coming back. Toward the end, she had told him not to grieve forever. He did what he dared not do. He looked down and again met Maureen's eyes—eyes that had always had such power over him.

"Please, Maureen, won't you have lunch with me before you leave? We'll catch up. It's been a long time since I saw you."

"I really should get back to the office."

He fell into step with her. "We'll make it a quick lunch. But we have a lot of catching up to do."

Allen chose a cozy table for two, sheltered by palm fronds, where the music was mellow and their conversation private. He waited until they ordered and then he blurted out, "Why didn't you wait for me, Maureen? I promised you the world and you weren't there when I came back with it in the palm of my hands."

For a moment Maureen couldn't speak. Then she said softly, "Allen, you came back looking for me?"

"Of course. I promised I'd come back, but you were gone."

"I thought you were dead, Allen."

He didn't seem to hear her. He peered around the flower vase. "I knocked on every door in the neighborhood. All they could tell me was that the Birklands pulled out in the middle of the night for Running Springs or Indiana."

Maureen shrank back at the memory, seared by the humiliation once again. Gone, she thought, before the neighbors discovered that the eldest Birkland child was in the family way, pregnant with a sailor's child, a disgrace to the stalwart Ellen Birkland.

He pushed the flower vase aside. "When I got back from the peacekeeping mission in Cyprus and found you gone, I was furious with you. I decided I'd never let a woman hurt me again."

He looked as though the wound was still raw, his dark eyes wistful, brooding. "Why did you go away, Reeny? You promised to wait for me."

"I did wait, Allen, until they told me you were dead."

He heard it this time. "Dead! Who told you that?"

She cut another slice of prime rib, her knife scratching the plate. "Don't you know?"

"I wouldn't ask if I did."

"Your father called me."

And before that, he had his lawyer send letters, she remembered. Finally he came himself to meet me. To buy me off—to make me leave you alone. And then that final call when he told me you had died in Cyprus. Dead on a peacekeeping mission.

She had forgotten how piercing Allen's gaze could be. "Your father told me that you had drowned. Why did he lie to me?"

"There was a serious accident when our landing craft went ashore on Cyprus. The United Nations representatives met with the Turks and Greeks on board our carrier." He retreated from her, came back, the food on his plate all but forgotten. "When their negotiations broke down, I was part of the crew assigned to escort the peacekeepers back to shore. We had almost reached land when we were fired on. We just disintegrated in the water—I was so scared."

Impulsively, she slid her arm across the table linen and put her hand over his. "Allen, I'm sorry."

"The explosion killed some of the men. The body of a friend dragged me under the water with him. Someone else pulled me up, locked his arm around my neck and towed me ashore."

"Who?"

"I don't know. I just remember waking up in an isolated encampment with Turks all around me. One twisted my dog tags around my neck, demanding answers I couldn't give him. I didn't know a thing about the secret negotiations on board the carrier. I favored the Greeks, of course, but I really didn't care who controlled Cyprus, as long as I could go home again. I wanted to get back to you."

She looked down at his hand. "But why did your father tell me you were dead?"

"For a time, he thought I was. He was told I was missing and presumed dead—several bodies unaccounted for." Allen's eyes were somber. "The Turks didn't release me for three months. They weren't unkind, but all I could think about was you. I was afraid you would think I had deserted you when you didn't hear from me."

"Why did your father let me go on grieving?"

"I wrote to you. My letters came back. Once our ship hit San Diego and I got shore leave, I headed right up the coast to your place. Where were you, Reeny?"

"With friends in Running Springs for a little while."

Cold shivers ran up her spine. *Meggy!* Tell him about Meggy. She had insisted that the baby be born in California where she first met Allen. Her mother had insisted that the baby be given up for adoption—and she had wanted desperately to please her again.

She withdrew her hand. He reached for hers, but she pulled away. "I finished high school in Running

Springs. Then Mother wanted to move back to Indiana before a new term began. My brothers hated me...well, hated moving back there."

"When I couldn't trace you—when you didn't keep your promise to wait for me—I went up to the mountains and spent my leave by that brook where I last saw you."

Where we made love, she thought.

"Months later, when I got my navy discharge, I headed back to Seattle. You were gone, but I had job security with Dad."

"And you went to university," she prompted. "And married?"

"Not until I was twenty-six. Adrian was a wonderful girl, Maureen. We had twelve good years together before she died."

"I heard—I'm sorry."

He gave her a ghost of a smile. "One day Adrian was well. A few months later—dead. From leukemia," he said before she could ask him. "It's been almost a year to the day since I lost her."

She allowed him a moment of silence to recover his composure and then asked, "Did you have children, Allen?"

"No. I always wanted a child."

You have one, she thought.

"We tried—Adrian and I. God knows, we tried." He lifted his tumbler and twirled the water. "It's what makes it so tough with Adrian gone. I've missed having a child more since she died—"

You *know,* she thought darkly. Somehow you know. You're trying to humiliate me. To make me confess that there is a child.

Allen went on. "Most men want a son, but I wanted a little girl who would grow up as beautiful and sweet-spirited as Adrian. Adrian was such an uncomplicated, open person." He pushed his unfinished dinner plate away and palmed his hands. "I hated military life so I didn't want a son running off to join the navy, or going off to war to defend some foreign oil field."

"Your son wouldn't have to join the navy. You only did it to get away from your father."

"And so I could marry you," he reminded her.

She looked away from his dark, unyielding eyes.

"But in the end your dad won."

"Yes, in spite of our differences. I finally went to work for him and carried my share of the load. He seemed pleased, but he expected a lot from his chosen successor." He shook his head. "Dad was a bear to live with. It was just my two brothers and me—and Mom always trying to patch up our differences. I guess that's one reason I wanted a daughter. Someone to love, not bicker with." He sat back, taking her in with a sweeping gaze. "But what about you, Reeny? I noted you have several degrees behind your name."

"A few." She flushed. What else had he noted?

"And you married? Of course, you're married. Your name is different now."

"Married briefly—and widowed."

It was his turn to say, "I'm sorry. What happened?"

She told him about Carl, about his fast-paced living, his racing, his death.

"I can't picture you with someone like that. Were you happy together?"

She felt a frown knit between her brows. "We were never totally unhappy. We had different schedules, different priorities," she admitted. "Different life-styles."

"Why did you stay with him, Reeny?"

She felt the color creep into her cheeks. "Divorce was

never an option with us. We married for keeps and we worked hard to make a go of it." When he didn't respond, she said, "I loved him, Allen. Carl was special. Fun to be with. He was good to me. But he expected me to be at his races and I dreaded that. I was always afraid something would happen to him."

"And it did?"

"Yes, I was at the race track the day he was killed."

"I'm sorry, Reeny."

"So was I."

He filled in the awkward silence, saying, "What about your mother? Or do I dare ask?"

"She makes her home in Indiana near one of the boys. They're good to her. All three of them."

"But living alone? So she's still as independent as ever?"

"She never changes. She sets high standards. You live up to them if you want to please her. I'm still trying to please her."

"I never did," Allen said.

"I guess you didn't, but then you weren't dating Mother."

That brought a smile to his face. "Funny," he said, "when I finally find you, you're a competitor. I never thought you were interested in the aircraft industry."

"I started out as a research scientist. Missiles mostly."

"Ouch. You are a competitor."

I don't want to be, she thought. "Allen, I know your wife's death was unbearable, but you've done well professionally. I'm glad you went to work for your father. It's what he always wanted."

"When I wasn't working, I was dating. Doing my best to wipe you from my mind. I did, too. When I thought no one permanent would come along, I met Adrian. In a way, she reminded me of you, Maureen. She always looked me in the eye the way you do.''

He paused briefly. ''Everything Adrian did, she did with her whole heart.''

Oh, Allen, she thought, after all these years apart you recognized me instantly. Yet you don't even see me, do you? I sit here listening to you talk about someone else and I hate it. But I understand. You need to talk. You need to put your life with Adrian to rest.

Allen took her silence as an invitation to go on. He said, ''Reeny, I met you when I was barely nineteen—still wet behind the ears—when my whole life was surfing the waves off the Huntington Beach Pier. I was twenty-six when I met Adrian, more mature, ready for marriage. It was different. You were different, Maureen. I guess I can say that you were my first love—''

''And Adrian was the love of your life?''

He looked grateful. ''Yes, she changed me, Reeny. She was very, very special.''

You told *me* that once, Maureen thought.

But she understood. Their romance had been quick, youthful, full of passion and promises, but with nothing stable to build their lives on. It had ended almost as abruptly as it had begun. She said, ''I'm glad. It sounds as if your years with Adrian were happy ones. Not everyone can say as much.''

He nodded. ''Yes, that's true. I loved her.''

For a moment she forgot the half-eaten meal and her anger over the pending merger. Her voice softened to a whisper, ''How are you doing, Allen? Really.''

''I'm okay. Better these last few days. I keep busy. But without Adrian, a part of me is still missing.''

If he didn't quit rubbing his hands, the skin would be

raw—those big smooth hands, a wedding band still on his left finger.

"Can I help, Allen?"

"How? The truth is, I still walk along the lake every week. That's where we spent so much of our time together. Nick says I'm crazy—that I ought to get on with my life. And I am trying. But I thought my life ended the day Adrian died."

She wanted to go to him, put her arms around his shoulders and comfort him. To tell him that someday he'd find happiness again. But she didn't want to start something she couldn't stop.

Maureen knew that he had slipped from her presence again, lost in his thoughts. He was suddenly back. "I should apologize to you, Reeny. Burdening you with my pain."

A crooked grin tugged at the corner of his mouth. "And then that brother of mine got a bit out of hand in the conference today. I should apologize for him, too."

"Why do you put up with it?"

"Nick and I never got on. Fought more with him than with Chris. I think it all had to do with the company. I was the eldest son—Dad's choice to replace him. Nick wanted that job."

"He still does," she guessed.

"What about you and Carl, Reeny? How did you meet?"

She twisted the opal on her ring finger—where she had once worn Carl Davenport's diamond and wedding band.

"My youngest brother introduced us, but Mother never approved. She never approved of any of the men in my life. She always called Carl a speed demon. She was right, of course. Carl was always the charming one, riding in the fast lane.''

"Tough," Allen said.

"On his family mostly. He lived fast. Died the same way.''

"Any children?''

Do I tell him? Yes, take the risk. He would consider it Carl's child. Her words were barely a whisper. "One. A girl.''

"Lucky you, Reeny. I'd like to meet her.''

A morsel of prime rib lodged in her throat. So would I, she thought. So would I.

"Does she look like you?''

She tried to recall that first impression when her infant daughter had lain in her arms, moments before she was taken away. The baby had long silken strands of raven hair, her skin dark like Allen's. Maureen had run her hand through the thick downy mop, touched the baby's soft cheeks, and run her finger over the closed eyelids until the lids blinked open.

Her eyes were blue, but then all babies have blue eyes, she thought. But perhaps they are dark like Allen's now. "She looks more like her father.''

"But you don't intend to introduce me.''

Tell him. Tell him the truth, said a voice inside.

But she couldn't. Wouldn't. Not yet. Perhaps not ever. "She may not want to meet you, Allen. I'd have to tell her about us. I'm not sure she'd understand.''

"What's there to tell? We loved each other, Reeny. There was nothing to be ashamed of.''

Really? she thought. You left me pregnant, unmarried.

"That argument didn't hold water with Mother," she replied.

"Your mother never did approve of me. But what's

wrong with telling your daughter that we're old friends?'' He shrugged. ''How old is she anyway?''

Tell him her real age and he'll guess the truth, she thought. Maybe not this moment, but later when he thinks about what I said. ''In her late teens,'' she said.

''Does she have a name?''

She would have named her Megan. She had even noted that on the paperwork when the adoption went through. Whenever she thought about her, she called her Meggy.

''Meggy,'' she said out loud.

''I have a feeling she's lovely like you, Maureen. You must be very proud of her.''

Chapter Eight

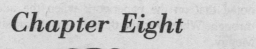

Lunch was over, but Allen was obviously reluctant to let her go. He walked her through the elegant lobby and held open the door as she stepped outside. She turned to say goodbye, and he was still there, smiling down at her. As they reached the garden walkway on the way to the parking lot, he said, "It's still early. Don't leave."

She glanced at her watch. "Eddie expects me back at the office."

"Call him."

She laughed. "And tell him what? That I've just had lunch with his chief competitor and we're still busy chatting. He would think I was already taking sides with Larhaven."

He tucked her arm in his. "Would that be so bad?"

"I've been with Fabian a long time, Allen. They've been good to me. Good advancements. Good benefits. Until recently I thought I had a future with them."

Her feet ached already, but she walked along the man-made lake to please him, circling it as they talked.

"I can see the lake from my room, Reeny. Reminds

me of home. My condo up north faces Lake Washington.''

"Nice.''

"We thought so when we bought it.''

Would it always be like that with Allen? Adrian slipping into the conversation unasked, uninvited? But always there. Part of him.

Of course. He had loved her.

He squeezed her fingers. "I'm still surprised at seeing you here. And pleased at how successful you've become. Your mother must be proud of you.''

"She's too busy being proud of my brothers.''

He backed off. "Eddie mentioned you were expecting to make CEO when he retired. His staying on must have been quite a blow.''

As the color crept into her cheeks, she looked away. "There had been talk of it. A pipe dream, as it turned out. And then everything changed when the merger plans went back on the board.''

He dealt with her silence for a few minutes. "I never dreamed you were part of Fabian, Maureen. You must know that.''

"Then I had the advantage. I knew your family owned Larhaven. There was kind of an irony to the takeover. But I thought you were dead, Allen. That your father was still at the helm.''

"Is that why you fought the merger?''

"Because of your father? No. I still thought Fabian could make a go of it and increase our profits enough to stay on top. We were in line for some good government contracts. And then—''

"Then McCormick got sick, and Fabian was in deep trouble.''

"You knew that?''

"Yes."

"Then you had an informer within our program," she accused.

"Yes, I guess you would call it that."

"Not Dwayne Crocker?"

"Would it matter?"

"We're friends. I'd hate to think that he betrayed Fabian."

A shadow passed across Allen's face. "Close friends?"

"Colleagues."

"Crocker approves of the merger, doesn't he?"

"He approves of anything that means money in his pocket."

Allen loosened his tie. "What would you have done if my father had still been on board?"

"Little probably. He didn't like women in leadership, so I knew my position would be threatened. But I wasn't worried about him recognizing me. Twenty years make a difference."

"He didn't change."

"But I did."

"Yes. You grew more beautiful and confident."

"And your father only saw me twice."

"Reeny, I'm sorry about all of that. My brother said—"

"Which brother? Nick?"

"Chris never interfered. Even now he has little interest in Larhaven. It's Nick who knows everything." He looked out at the water, his expression grim, pained. "Nick said my father bought you off," he said, without emotion.

He knows, she thought, panicking. He knows about

Meggy. "I don't know what you're talking about, Allen."

"Nick said Dad paid you to not see me again."

Her lips tightened. "He couldn't have paid me enough to stay away from you. Really, Allen, I must go."

"I'm sorry. I had to know. I never understood why you weren't there when I went back for you."

"I told you—I thought you were dead."

He stopped and faced her. "I loved you, Reeny. Things worked out for me. I met Adrian years later. I was happy. But I never understood why you didn't wait for me."

"We were just a couple of kids, Allen. Immature."

"Are you saying there was nothing between us?"

She tried to pull free, but he wouldn't let her. "It was so long ago, Allen. How do you expect me to remember?"

"I remembered everything the minute you walked into that conference this morning. You did, too. I saw it in your eyes."

"Embarrassment, perhaps. Nothing more." Her heart was out-of-control, beating wildly. "Thank you for lunch, Allen. Now I really must go."

She whirled around so fast that she bumped into him. He reached out to steady her. "What about dinner tonight, Reeny? You name the place."

She was hurrying now, heading for the parking lot. Allen kept pace with her hurried steps.

"What about dinner?" he asked again.

The thought of dressing up and going out to eat again was more than she wanted to consider. Impulsively, she offered, "Why don't we have dinner at my place?"

He looked pleasantly surprised. "I'd like that."

Would *she?* The invitation was out. She could not withdraw it. "What about eight o'clock?"

"You won't be too tired?"

"I have to eat. And now I must get back to the office. I'm still employed, you know."

He winced and covered his embarrassment. "Can I bring something for supper?"

"Yourself, Allen."

When they reached her car, a new worry struck her. She asked hesitantly, "What about your brother?"

His brows arced, a remembered expression catching him off guard. "Nick is a big boy now. He can fend for himself."

Good, she thought, glad that he would not be joining them.

He opened the car door for her and she slipped into the driver's seat. He leaned in the window. "Until eight then."

She gave him a quick wave and was off. As she turned out of the hotel driveway, she glanced in her mirror. Allen was still standing there, his hands jammed in his pockets, watching her.

On her way home from work, she stopped off at the market for fresh salmon and the makings of a salad. She couldn't fix Allen's favorite meal—she had no idea what it was—so she chose one of her own. She realized later, as she tossed the salad and topped it with asparagus tips and sliced hard-boiled eggs, that she knew little about Allen. His likes and dislikes. His favorite foods. His favorite books. His habits. His hobbies.

Twenty years ago they had feasted on hamburgers and fries drenched in ketchup, and on hot dogs cooked over an open fire on the beach. In all the time she knew him, they had never sat down to a meal at home or dined at a fancy restaurant. And now she wondered whether he would be easy to please.

She set the table with her best china, thinking that she was not used to setting the table for two. It was always for an even six: friends and business associates. For the most part she ate alone in her kitchen, half the time standing at the counter. She had never needed to diet, but enjoyed simple breakfasts and fruits and vegetables and fish for the main meal. Roasts were out. Who wanted to cook a roast for one?

She had just filled the crystal goblets with ice water when the doorbell rang. Her oven was already turned on, but she took time to pop the salmon fillets in to bake. They were pink and fresh with herb butter, diced onion and lemon slices on top.

The bell rang again as she made her way toward the door. She swung it open, smiling. Allen had dressed casually: dark slacks and a short-sleeved beige shirt. He thrust a bouquet of red roses into her hands, looking suddenly uncomfortable and boyish as he stepped into the parquet entryway.

"I hope I'm not late."

"You're early. It gives me just enough time to slip these into some water."

"I couldn't remember your favorite flowers."

"I don't think you ever knew."

"Adrian loved roses."

"Most women do," she said without malice.

As she disappeared from the room with the flowers in her hands, Allen glanced around. He expected the condo to be buzzing with the sounds of a teenager, or some signs of her presence. But the place seemed empty, the music subdued and classical.

He prowled, his feet sinking comfortably into the white rug. The place was tastefully decorated with expensive furnishings—a baby grand in one corner and a Renoir print on the wall. He found one photo on the piano: a young girl on a horse, her face not clearly seen because of the riding helmet. He guessed it to be Meggy and tried to imagine a likeness to Maureen's features—but saw none. Maureen was back in the room now, the vase of flowers in her hands. She put them on the coffee table.

"They're lovely, Allen. Thank you."

"Meg?" he asked, nodding at the photograph.

"No, a friend's daughter."

She offered no further explanation, but was back moments later with a serving trolley, loaded with good foods.

"Smells good," he said.

"If you like salmon."

"I come from salmon country." He bit his tongue, stopping himself in time from bragging about Adrian's salmon casserole. He lit the candles for Maureen as she placed the plates of buttered green beans and steaming rice on the table.

"I think we're ready, Allen."

He thought he was stuffed from lunch, but ate heartily. Maureen had matured in a lot of ways, and her ability to cook was one of them. It was easy to be with her again, and, once started, they never ran out of conversation. Her phone rang once during dessert, and she answered it curtly and abruptly. Again he felt troubled.

"Meg?" he asked when she severed the call.

"No. Dwayne Crocker."

He didn't want to pursue that one, but he moved to the living room gladly when she invited him to leave the dishes. She said she would take care of them in the morning, but he knew her well enough to know that once he went out the door, she would tackle the task before retiring.

He sank onto the white divan, his back pressed against the teal cushion. The room was vibrant, alive with Maureen's creativity. "Come on, Maureen. Sit down with me. Relax a bit. It's been a big day."

She nodded and slipped down gracefully on the opposite end of the divan. Their eyes met across the length of the sofa.

I still love you, he thought. "I can't believe my good fortune, finding you again after all these years."

"I've been here all along. Or almost all that time."

Moments later he slid across the sofa and caught her in the curve of his arm. He sat there without talking, holding her gently, feeling no resistance.

Old longings rose within him, the beat of his heart throbbing wildly. Allen tilted her chin up and saw in her velvet-lashed eyes that her desire matched his own. He leaned down and pressed his lips hard against hers. It seemed but yesterday since he held her this way. He felt the same now—captivated by the softness of her cheek against his, enamored by the sweet scent of her perfume. Abruptly he released her and sat back.

For a second their eyes held. She was vulnerable, beautiful. He touched her cheek as a ribbon of crimson settled there. More than anything he wanted to stay, but he said hastily, "I'd better be going. There's a full day at Fabian tomorrow."

"Don't remind me."

"Nick and I are staying on a couple of extra days. I

want to go over the missile project with you and—I've made plans for us on Saturday, if you can get away.''

He waited, fearing that he was rushing her. If she did, he was going to suggest that they make it a threesome and take her daughter along.

''What do you have in mind?'' Maureen asked.

He grinned. ''How about cycling along the coast?''

''Like we used to do?''

So she remembered. ''Are you free?''

''Yes, I have no obligations.''

No obligations. So she lived alone. There was no sign of a teenager around here and even after the meal, when he excused himself and went upstairs to the bathroom, there was nothing of Meg's about. No hair dryer left plugged into the outlet. No wet towel plopped on the floor. Just two bedrooms—one obviously a guest room.

Perhaps she was away at boarding school. Or living elsewhere. But why? Were Maureen and her daughter estranged? The other bedroom was the master room, looking feminine and very much like Maureen. He had come here this evening expecting to meet Maureen's daughter, but wherever she was, she did not live here.

And not with her father. Maureen's husband had died five years ago. There were no pictures, either. And then a dark thought crossed his mind. Surely Meg was not living in Cedar Lake, Indiana, with her grandmother....

''You look troubled, Allen. What's wrong? Have you forgotten how to ride a bike?''

''No.'' But I'd almost forgotten how much you once meant to me, he thought. He stood abruptly.

''Maureen, I really must get back to the hotel before I forget my way.''

Before I take you into my arms again.

Chapter Nine

On Sunday evening Maureen sat curled in her swivel recliner in the living room, a writing pad balanced on her lap. Seven sheets of rose-scented stationery lay crumpled in tight round balls on the floor beside an envelope already stamped and addressed to Mrs. Ellen Birkland in Cedar Lake, Indiana.

Maureen felt the brisk night air sweep through a nearby window. There was another chill inside her, a numbing apprehension. What if her mother learned about the merger between Larhaven and Fabian in the business pages of the newspaper, or saw the smiling face of Allen Kladis flashed across the screen on the television news? She could predict her mother's reaction: shock that Allen was alive, irritation with Maureen, and then she'd be out to her broker buying the usual ten shares of stock in the new company.

In spite of her interest in current events and her dabbling in investments, her mother refused to read letters typed on Maureen's computer. "How do I know whether your secretary wrote your letter for you or not? You and your busy schedule!''

Maureen thought, If it weren't for my busy schedule, Mother, you wouldn't have so much money in the bank, month after month.

Her mother never asked if Maureen sent it. If she credited anyone, it would be one of her three fine sons—Maureen's younger brothers. The grown boys that never displeased her. A monthly bank transfer was a small price to pay for the debt that Maureen still owed her mother.

The twenty-year-old wound between them remained ragged and raw, healing out of reach. They didn't get on emotionally and hadn't since Maureen was in high school. Yet they could chat amiably about the weather and politics and the aerospace industry. In her own way, Ellen Birkland kept abreast of Maureen's career and promotions and even boasted of them. But Maureen could not remember when she last went home on a holiday. They settled for letters, brief calls and between-plane visits at airports when Maureen traveled on business. They just couldn't stay in the same room for any length of time without the sins of Maureen's youth creeping into the conversation.

Her frugal mother—a carefully groomed, gray-haired woman who carried herself confidently, made friends easily, had a flare for the culinary—was a steady church-goer, more concerned with Maureen's sins than her own. The unforgiving curve of Ellen's mouth and her disapproving comments always spoiled their reunions.

It was not that Maureen did not want to be friends. As a child, she had adored her mother, and even now wanted to be strong like her. But her own bitterness sparked whenever her mother said, "I wanted marriage and children for you, Maureen."

"But I did marry. I *did* have a child."

To her mother, neither counted. She had not approved of Carl Davenport's flamboyant ways and never overcame the humiliation of Maureen bearing a child out of wedlock. When Maureen's mother counted grandchildren, "Meggy" was never added in.

How many years? Maureen wondered. How many lifetimes must I keep paying for the birth of my child? She had tried to earn her mother's respect and approval. She wanted Ellen Birkland to be proud of her and longed to erase the feud between them.

But it was you, Mother, who insisted that we give my baby away. And you—you speak of a forgiving God, yet you refuse to forgive me.

Mother, she agonized, I was only seventeen when I loved Allen Kladis. And what about now? she asked herself.

She allowed her gaze to stray around the living room with its posh interior and thick soft carpet. Each intricate detail from the Impressionist print on the wall to the elegant modern furniture revealed Maureen's artistic flair and good taste.

She could never afford the prices for an original painting at Sotheby's or Christie's, but she settled for reproductions of her favorite artists, often seeing herself portrayed in their images. She was gracious and sociable in the casual ways like that depicted in Renoir's boating party, and ached to be free like the woman on the swing in Fragonard's painting.

But she was modern, too, and unconventional. She chose to keep her exercise bike in the corner that faced the giant television, and across the room from it sat

Carl's baby grand piano where she still spent so many hours of pleasure. During her marriage to Carl, he had insisted on music with a quick tempo. Mostly he thrived on the old rock 'n' roll favorites.

Thankfully, Allen liked his music soft and romantic. With a flush to her cheeks, her eyes settled on the white, Wingate divan where Allen had sat last evening watching her. At one in the morning, he had stood abruptly, apologizing for the lateness of the hour. She had not gone with him to the door, but afterwards she had walked over, leaned against it and wept.

How do I tell Mother? she asked herself again, her thoughts coming back to the unfinished letter. Do I dare tell her that I spent time with Allen Kladis—starting with lunch at his hotel? Her mother would misinterpret this one, and send her silent accusations across the miles. Then again, why should Maureen spoil Saturday's tandem bicycle ride with Allen along the Pacific Coast by sharing it with the one person who would not welcome Allen into her home?

Dear Mother, she wrote and paused, chewing on the end of her pen. She tried again. She had picked the phone up twice to tell her about Allen, but she could not bear hearing the scathing in her mother's voice. *"Allen still alive? Really?"*

Yet, despite the recriminations Maureen was sure would come, she felt compelled to tell her mother the news.

She took another sheet of scented stationery and scratched a one-page note to her mother. This time she wrote quickly: *I had lunch with Allen Kladis on Wednesday. Yes, Allen is alive, and I will see him again in the morning.*

* * *

Allen arrived at Maureen's apartment early Monday morning to drive her to work. She was up and dressed in her red silk business suit, with her attaché case on the recliner table, when the chimes rang.

She went slowly, primping en route, not wanting him to know that the teenager still trapped inside her wanted to run to the door. She prayed that he would not notice how eager she was to see him. But when she flung back the door, Allen was obviously not ready for work. He stood there, tall and handsome, grinning down at her—but casually dressed in slacks and a blue Shetland sports shirt. As she saw him sweep back strands of hair from his forehead, she realized the grief shadows in his dark eyes were gone.

"Allen," she said, "Fabian has an iron-clad dress code."

The lines at the corners of his mouth dimpled. "Don't look so worried," he said, stepping inside. "I told Eddie McCormick that Nick would be there—suit and all—but you and I had some business to tend to before I left Orange County."

"Business? We can't discuss the missile contracts in public, or drive out to the Wallingdale Air Base without notifying them."

"Don't worry. I didn't bring a road map. I have something else in mind. You know, sharing a peach milk shake for old time's sake."

"With two straws?"

"More fun that way." He rocked on his white running shoes.

"Allen, I can't just not show up at work. And I can't call in this late to request a free day."

"I've already called for you. Besides, Eddie really thinks we have business matters to tend to."

"Oh, Allen."

"No arguments. We only have today," he said wistfully.

"Then you are leaving?"

"You knew I would."

She had put it out of her mind. "So soon."

"Too soon," he agreed. "I have a ton of work in Seattle. It looks like Larhaven won the toss over that mid-west company."

"Nick said you would."

Allen nodded. "Nick suggests—and I think he's right—that given time, we should bid on that company, too. Merge with them."

You're ambitious like your father, she thought. And yet he seemed like the old Allen: fair and considerate. "Another sixteen-billion-dollar merger! Can you afford it?"

"We're in a good position financially. Work is about the only place these days where my optimism still shines through." Except, his eyes seemed to say, when I'm with you. "I've told Nick to look into it. Now, come on, Reeny. Change into something comfortable and let's get going. I'll give you five minutes."

He strode across the room and dropped easily onto the divan, sitting with his arms stretched out, his hands flat against the cushions.

"But where are we going, Allen?"

"I told you. We're going for a milk shake. I have my rental in the driveway, ready to roll."

She felt uneasy again, afraid to trust herself alone with him when Wednesday evening stayed so vividly in her mind. Did she really want to be with Allen all day?

How? Why? she wondered. To you I am just a date, she thought, an old acquaintance. To me, you are everything—everything even down to the thudding beat of my heart. "Have you had breakfast?" she asked, still uncertain. "I could make some for both of us."

"No delays. Go on, change. We don't want to waste a minute."

Still she hesitated. She was a woman of responsibility, not given to impulsive behavior. But this was Allen.... "You're certain you cleared it with Eddie? He always has so many questions."

"I've already fielded them for you."

"You're sure, Allen?"

"As sure as I've ever been in my life."

As they rode along the coast highway, Maureen stole glances at Allen. He breathed in the salt-drenched air and pointed to the surfers on the azure water, sparkling now as the sun broke through the diaphanous veils of morning fog. "Reeny, look at those breakers and those maniacs riding them. Lucky guys! I've missed this."

The waves crested and broke, one on top of the next, each new wave erasing the one before it. The surfers rose from their boards to ride the eight-foot whitecaps. The rollers tumbled forward, crashing and roaring as they broke, pummeling the surfboarders beneath the surface. Their energy spent, the breakers turned into ribboned shreds as they rolled to shore and back with the tide again.

"Do you still surf, Allen?"

"Haven't for years. About the only thing I do now is surf the Internet."

She looked out to where the clouds and the sea mirrored each other. Billowing white puffs touched the rising sea—the spumy, foamy, waves. "You always liked riding the waves," she said.

"Not much opportunity for that in Seattle."

"I thought you'd never outgrow it."

"That's what my father said. I still have my old board packed away in a storage shed at the plant."

"The shed where you carved our initials?"

He looked genuinely surprised. "I'd forgotten about that. I did, didn't I? Your initials and mine—and the word forever under them." He rubbed his ear. "Forever wasn't very long, was it?"

It could have been, she answered silently, if your father hadn't betrayed us.

Allen seemed energized as they parked the car. He grabbed her hand and ran down the cement steps to the sandy beach, amber-gold in the morning sun. He grinned as they took the last step. "It's right around here." The smile wiped from his face. "Reeny, what happened to the food concession?"

"They must have torn it down."

"But our peach milk shake!" He waved his hand in disgust. "Destroyed it—just to make room for all these new shops?"

"It's called progress, Allen."

"I liked it better without those fancy hotels and stores." He shrugged, grinning again. "I think I spotted a burger shop across the street. Will you settle for a vanilla milk shake?"

"Yes. And two straws," she reminded him.

He took a step, then turned around. "Will you wait for me?"

Where else would she go? She smiled to reassure him. Why would she want to leave? This was the beach— almost the very spot—where she first met Allen. She had thought him athletic and strong in his royal-blue wet suit. And handsome with that lock of dark hair falling over his forehead and those deep brown eyes unblinking as he turned and saw her. He had stood barefoot in the sand, holding a milk shake in his hand. She blushed when his eyes met hers, but she'd been bold, too, not wanting him to walk away.

She sat on the sand in the shadow of the pier and hugged her knees as she waited now for Allen to come back. She listened to the roaring breakers and watched the men in wet suits paddle out to meet the challenge of the next giant wave.

Once it had been Allen out there in a wet suit, flexing his muscles, lying on his board, propelling himself out to meet the waves. Waiting and watching for just the right one—and at just the right moment catching a crest and riding it to shore. Watching the crashing surf, watching and remembering, her heartbeat out of sync, her emotions roiling and swelling with the tide, her very self swallowed up by nostalgia and the deep longing for Allen to love her as he once had.

Allen slipped down beside her, as quietly as the wind blew across the waters. "It's beautiful here," he said, popping two straws into the milk shake. "Thank you for coming back here with me."

They faced each other, their foreheads touching as they sipped. "Pretend it's peach," he said between swallows.

Pretend that it's twenty years ago, she told herself. *Pretend!* Why must she always pretend? She loved this man—had always loved him. Did he not see her emotions naked, raw, exposed before him? She wanted to see more in his eyes than flecks of black shadows, or his gaze shifting from kindness to wariness. He was on the edge, drawing her back in time. But she wanted to snatch at this moment, to make him see her now, not yesterday.

Adrian's name had not even been mentioned, yet his wife hung between them like a storm cloud. Allen, Allen, she thought, I know that you miss her, but she's gone. *I'm here.*

Allen took the last few swallows of the milk shake and sat back, twisting the straw, his face suddenly pensive. And then a string of Allen's "Maureen, do you remember?" filled the space between them, his memories then interrupted by her own.

And they'd laugh and start over, neither one voicing a comment about that last time together. The horrible row with Maureen's mother. Running off in Allen's battered old car. The commitments made on that camping trip. Allen's news that he had joined the navy.

An hour or two passed before Allen said, "Do you realize neither one of us has mentioned Big Bear."

"I know," she whispered, "but I've never liked goodbyes."

"I never meant for it to be forever."

"Isn't that what you wrote on your board?"

"I would never have met you, Reeny, if I hadn't come south that spring." He swept the area with his hand. "You were standing just about there the first time I saw you. Do you realize how beautiful you were that day?"

Have I changed much? she wondered.

He touched her face, his hand still cold from holding the milk shake; it cooled her burning cheeks. "Maureen, you are still so very lovely—and your eyes more lovely than ever."

"Violet-blue," she teased.

"They always blew me away."

"And now?" she wanted to ask, but didn't dare.

He drew back suddenly and looked out at the water. With a deep sigh, he pushed himself to his feet and pulled her up beside him.

"Where to?" she asked warily, brushing sand from her hands.

"What did we do the day we met?"

She remembered. Didn't *he?* "We kicked off our shoes and walked in the waves and talked and we ate candy bars out on the end of the pier because we didn't have enough money for lunch." *And we fell in love and we held hands and we kissed good-night,* she wanted to add.

"Lunch! Sounds like a plan."

Shafts of sunlight blinded them as they walked to the end of the pier. Ruby's, the restaurant sign said. It was a white building with a red octagonal roof and fifties' music coming from inside.

"That's new, isn't it, Reeny?"

"Yes. The old restaurant was swallowed up in a storm."

"Like Jonah?" he asked, glancing down at her.

"A fish took Jonah down, if I remember correctly. But the pilings beneath us are supposed to be quite sturdy."

He guided her inside to a booth that overlooked the ocean. The young waitress was dressed in a style from the fifties—a red gingham uniform with a white hat and apron. As they ate the lush hamburgers and chips, and drank cherry cokes, they watched a half-dozen men and boys on the dock casting their lines and scaling their catch.

Allen turned back and smiled, his reserve melting away again. "I love the ocean, Reeny. It's got a hold on me. Maybe we ought to sail away and see the world.

Just the two of us.'' But the swell of happiness she felt at his invitation was flattened when he added, "We used to sail a lot in Seattle.''

You and Adrian, she thought. Dead, but she stands between us.

When they left the restaurant, Allen took her toward the iron railing to watch the surfers defy nature. The whitecaps crashed onto the sandy shore. Beyond Ruby's and the end of the pier lay a tranquil-looking ocean, wind-rippled with pools of azure and aquamarine, and a pocket of Venetian blue where dolphins were diving and gliding. Distant mountains drew their own dividing line between sky and sea.

"It's an imposing view, isn't it?''

"Intoxicating, gripping,'' she breathed.

Was she describing the ocean, or these moments with Allen? She was not certain, but she savored them and thrilled to the touch of his sun-bronzed arm as it slipped across her shoulders.

Later, he held her hand as they kicked off their shoes and ran in the water, then walked for miles along the packed surf. As the day wore on, the sun and sky changed their colors. Maureen's skin went from a faint pink to a fire-red, and the ocean changed its rhythm from tigerish and frenzied to placid and serene. Yet its motion remained uncurbed; its mysterious mood lulled them with its infinite power. Maureen's spirit vacillated throughout the day—utter joy at just being with Allen, sadness, excitement, harmony and doubt. In the silence that had overtaken Allen, she knew that he had gone as far as he could for now, and she was content to simply be with him. He had not mentioned his wife's name, but Maureen knew that his mind and heart were still filled with Adrian's memory. She understood and sympathized.

Yet today as they beachcombed—or was it only wishful thinking?—Allen seemed more aware of Maureen, alive and walking at his side.

Give Allen time, she thought. Perhaps…

She had no guarantees, no promises. Yet in the weeks ahead, she would cling to the joys of their time together today. If this was all that could be, ever would be, she'd still be grateful. For too long, she'd survived on the memories of days twenty years past with all their remembered pain. But now, she had today. And she knew that the one thing that remained constant was her love for Allen.

As night fell and the sun set, they sat down on a log close to the water. Other couples sat nearby, murmuring softly, silhouetted by the shadows. In spite of them, Maureen and Allen were in a cocoon of their own, awed as they watched their day shutting down for the night. To Maureen, it looked like a kindergarten class had brushed wide strokes across the sky. Day had left a backdrop of blue behind. Leaden gray-and-black clouds formed long streamers, interspersed with rippled pink streaks. And as she watched the place where sky and sea met, a fiery mist of orange and gold changed to flaming red. Within seconds, the sun slipped behind the scarlet red ribbons, plunging the sky into darkness, and leaving only the sound of the lapping sea.

Now Maureen could see only the silhouette of the mountains in the distance. Even as he sat beside her, Allen's features were hidden by the darkness. They sat in the quiet of the night, their shoulders touching, saying nothing. Maureen was afraid to break the silence, dreading that Allen would say that they had to go.

Deep inside she yearned for Allen to take her in his arms again. At last he pulled her to him, his lips brushing the tip of her ear and settling lightly on her lips. His mouth was warm, his skin scented with ocean air.

She rested her cheek contentedly against his shoulder, but tears pricked her eyes as Allen said, "You've been so good for me these last few days, Reeny. And especially today, you've helped me find my way back, and enjoy life again."

So that was all it was, and all that this marvelous day had meant to him. Allen finding his way back—not finding *her* again.

He stood and brushed the sand from his hands, then reached out in the darkness and pulled her to her feet. "We'd better be going. My plane leaves early in the morning." He slipped his arm around her waist as they walked to his car. "I won't see you in the morning, Reeny, but today has just been perfect for me."

Not for us? she longed to ask.

She could hear the smile in his voice. "Thanks for making everything so special. I'm just sorry that I didn't get to meet that daughter of yours. Next time, maybe."

She wondered whether he would be back. And if he did come again, would it merely be to finalize the paperwork for the merger? The newness of seeing her would be gone by then, his therapeutic need of her forgotten.

It was a twenty-minute drive to her condo and her apprehension of their parting was as shattering as it had been that day he left for Cyprus. As they drove in silence, a canopy of darkness settled over her, its void creating a heaviness in her chest. That first time when he went away, she had expected to see him again. This time, did she dare dream that if and when he returned, their relationship would ever be more?

When Allen pulled up in front of her apartment complex, she said, "Don't get out, Allen." She was already out of the car. "It's late. I'll see myself in. And thanks—thanks for that little trip down memory lane."

He had his hand on the door, the key out of the ignition.

"Don't. Please," she insisted. "We're both tired."

"I could go for a cup of coffee," he said quietly. She heard surprise and confusion in his voice.

"Some other time, Allen." She ran blindly up the steps, the door key in her hand. She did not turn around, but she heard Allen shift into gear and drive away, the wheels squealing as he accelerated at the corner.

Maureen shuddered as the sound of Allen's car died away. She had sent him away, steeling herself against the pain of saying goodbye, protecting herself from what might have happened. If he had touched her, kissed her, she would not have been able to bear it. She loved him, but she did not want him to know.

For Allen, these few days had been part of his recovery from losing Adrian. She was not certain that he could even distinguish the difference between needing her companionship or simply finding comfort in her presence. For Maureen, it was not enough. She had been in over her head and now she knew that it had to end where it had started—with letting him go away. She could not call him back, even for a moment. She had allowed too many hours and days to slip by without telling him the truth. Without telling him about their daughter.

When she left Fabian, she would go with her head held high. She had at least two months left on the job, and then it would be time to send out her resume. She would disappear from Allen's life the same way he had once slipped from hers. With her job almost over, her hope of buying her dream home on the Pacific Ocean was out. She would call the real estate agent tomorrow and withdraw her bid. A home of her own was out of reach now, thanks to Allen's merger. And Cedar Lake was a long way away, but she had always wanted to go back to the home of her childhood. Perhaps she would.

Chapter Ten

At John Wayne Airport, Nick went off to handle the luggage and ticketing at the counter, leaving Allen moodily pacing in the lobby. They had been up since five, and three times he had the phone in his hand and three times he had jammed it back in place. He had wanted to hear Maureen's voice once more, to talk out their differences, to apologize for roaring off last evening. But it was Reeny who had cut *him* off, refusing to let him see her to her door. Things had been going well. So what happened? Why her quick retreat?

Had the Fabian–Larhaven merger come between them? In another month or two she would be out of a job, her high-paying position and hopes of promotion wiped out by the arrival of his own management team. But didn't she understand? He hadn't meant to hurt her—didn't even know she was working at Fabian. When he had told her that he could find her a job in the northwest—that they would work something out—her chin had jutted forward, the taut lines around her curved mouth deepening. He had blown it.

"Do you have the time, sir?"

Disturbed, he looked up into the face of a young man with a letterman's jacket stretched over his broad shoulders. Allen blinked, then checked his watch. "Six-twenty, to the second," he said.

Allen expected the stranger to be satisfied and leave him alone with his own dismal thoughts. But he was not to get out of it so easily. The young man went on amiably, "I was in such a rush to get here in time, I left my watch in the bathroom."

Allen didn't care where the man had left his watch. But he forced his attention back on the stranger. He was in his late twenties, his dark eyes wide-set, his blond hair thick. He was not handsome, but had strength in his expression and warmth in his grin. There was little to do but smile back.

"You'll miss your timepiece on your trip," Allen told him.

"Actually I'm meeting my girl—my fiancée. She's coming in from Indiana."

Allen checked the flight board. "I thought this flight was coming from Denver, going on to Seattle."

"I know. My girl works for the airline. She was back in Indiana and then on the Chicago–Denver run. She caught the first flight out of there back to John Wayne. But don't worry, the plane's going on to Seattle from here."

"Good," Allen said. "You had me stymied for a minute."

"The name's Brett, sir."

"Allen."

They shook hands, and he found Brett's grasp firm, confident. The young man's thoughts were still on his girl. "I've really missed Heather."

"Has she been gone long?"

The grin turned sheepish. "Five days. We're getting married in August."

"Good luck," Allen said sincerely. The boy looked so young. But hadn't *he* been about the same age when he'd been so determined to marry Maureen?

Maybe he should call Maureen. Try to explain about the job offer. Just say goodbye again. Suddenly, he was seized by the need to simply hear her soft voice.

"I need to make a phone call," he told Brett as he abruptly turned. "But good luck to you."

"Thanks," Brett replied with a smile and a wave.

Allen waved back and quickly crossed the corridor, weaving his way through the crowd.

He pulled out his wallet, flipping it open to his calling card. Hurriedly he plugged in the card and fed in Maureen's number. It rang.

"Come on. Come on, Maureen. Answer."

On the fifth ring her answering machine kicked in. He heard her voice—soft, professional, cool—saying, "Please leave a message...."

He hung up, turned back and ran. His flight was boarding, the waiting area nearly empty. Down the long corridor he spotted Brett in his letterman jacket, head and shoulders above his girl, his arm securely around her shoulders. She was smiling up at him, her long black hair falling softly around her shoulders.

As they strolled along, Brett's grip tightened around Heather's shoulders. "How did the trip to Indiana go?"

"It's over," she said in a small, tight voice.

"Did you get to Cedar Lake?"

He felt her shoulder stiffen. "It was a false lead. If the Jason Birklands ever lived there, they're gone now."

"It may have been the wrong Jason Birklands."

"I did find a cemetery plot nearby with a Jason Birkland buried there. He would be seventy now. But it didn't tell me anything else. It didn't tell me where his widow lived, or where his children might have gone. Whether he had a daughter—"

When her voice cracked, he asked, "Did you check the hospitals, sweetheart?"

"Cedar Lake is not that big—ten thousand maybe. St. Anthony Medical Center is six miles away in a place called Crown Point." She looked defeated. "Chicago is at least thirty-five miles away, but you know how many hospitals they have there. My mother could have been born in any one of them. I called three. But the minute they found I was looking for my birth mother, it was a closed book."

Brett felt the agitation in her quick, deliberate steps. "I called every Birkland I could find in the phone book in all the surrounding towns. Most of them were kind, but when one woman found out what I wanted, she slammed the phone in my ear."

Her chin quivered. "I dialed the number right back and a young man answered. Said he was Jason Birkland and didn't know anything about Running Springs or me. And he told me not to bother them again. Maybe he was Jason Birkland, Jr."

"Maybe you went about it the wrong way, honey."

She stopped abruptly. The swarming crowd surged around them. "I don't understand you, Brett. It's my *life*. I have a right to know. I don't want to wonder the rest of my days who I am."

She had discarded her fight attendant's uniform in Denver and was wearing a light-weight turtleneck sweater, white against her slender neck. He hadn't realized how drained of color she had been in these last few weeks. "Honey, we can talk about it later."

"No. Now. I've lived with it alone for far too long. These last five days have been unbearable. Even on the flight to Denver, the passengers would ask me something, and I wasn't hearing them. I wasn't doing my job, Brett. All I could think about was me."

"Hush," he said gently, brushing her hair back from her face. Taking her elbow, he edged her toward the wall.

"I'm right here with you, sweetheart. I'm listening. I love you. Don't ever forget that."

Her eyes glistened with tears. "I felt so alone in Cedar Lake. I went to the county's Vital Statistics Office and spent hours there. For nothing. I could only guess at the year of my mother's birth. If I had her actual birth date...her social security number...I might be able to find her."

"No Birklands recorded there?"

"Dozens of them. Most of them boys. Three girls. Susan Maureen. Abigal Joy. And a tongue twister: Tabitha Sabrina. There were no Birklands by those names in the phone book."

"Maybe they married," he suggested.

"And no way for me to trace them. No matter where I turned, Brett, the adoption records were sealed. No one can open them without good cause."

"Our getting married wasn't cause enough?"

She smiled through her tears. "I don't think I mentioned that—Brett, I don't know what I'd do without you."

"Then you can't shut me out. You have to let me help you."

"I can't let you get behind in your studies."

"I'm a basket case at the seminary already—especially in my Old Testament class on Lamentations. I'm like the weeping prophet thinking about you."

"You can't do that and pass."

"And you can't go striking out on your own. Grabbing at straws. You have to narrow it down, Heather. You're jumping in too hard. Too fast. Flying off to Indiana like that."

"What did you expect me to do? That lady in Running Springs said she was certain the Birklands moved back to Cedar Lake."

"But were you born there?"

Her cry was a wail. "I don't know where I was born. You know, Brett. When I was growing up, kids used to talk about where they were born. Who was there. I don't know those things. I can't go to the hospital where I was born and say, 'This is the place.' Lately, I can't even be certain what city I was born in. Or even the hour of my birth. I don't know whether I had grandparents. Or whether my father knew about me before he died in Cyprus."

"I guess I've always taken knowing such things for granted."

"Yes, Brett, and I envy you. All I know is that my birth mother may have been born near Cedar Lake."

He leaned back and butted his head against the wall in frustration. "But you don't know that for certain."

"That's all Mom and Dad remember about my birth mother. But they know I was born here in California. And Dad pulled Running Springs out of a hat, and then couldn't remember why. That's why I went up the mountain to check it out. And I learned precious little, except that my mother was young and very pretty."

"I can believe that. You're beautiful." He took her

hand in his and held it tightly. "Tonight—or by this weekend at the latest—we're going to sit down with Todd and Nan and ask them to tell us everything they remember. And we're going to work from there."

"I don't want to hurt them."

"It's hurting you, not knowing. From now on, I expect you to let me help you. No more running off anywhere without me. We're going to get to the bottom of this together. And, Heather, if your mother lived here in California, that's where I'd start."

"I just thought Cedar Lake was the place to start."

"We may end up going back there. I'd like to talk to that Jason Birkland myself. We'll see."

As they headed for the baggage area to collect her luggage, she looked up and whispered, "Brett, I wonder if my mother ever grieved for me?"

"It had to be hard," he said seriously. "She was letting you go forever. It couldn't have been easy on her."

"She might have been a very hard woman."

"And be your biological mother? Not likely. I know Todd and Nan raised you, but something of your birth parents is deep inside of you. And, Heather, you are a very kind and gentle person."

"You're sweet."

"You know that I love you." He reached out and grabbed one of her suitcases from the spinning turnstile. "Whatever happens, I'm here for you."

"Do you think my birth mother ever thinks of me?"

"Heather, it's possible that she's not even alive."

She trembled visibly. "Do you think she ever loved me?"

"I don't know, Heather. She could not have let you go without some feeling for you."

"Guilt?"

"I was thinking more of love. Of wanting the best for you."

"Is it so wrong to want to know what my roots are?"

"Only you can answer that, sweetheart. It only matters to me because it is important to you. I can go on without ever knowing…. But I don't think you can."

Chapter Eleven

Maureen slid off the piano bench and stood in the middle of the living room trying to attach importance to dusting and cooking, but finding stomach for neither. Her thoughts were on her daughter and had been for days, ever since Allen stormed back into her life. She had not told Allen the truth about Meggy. But what could she tell him? "Allen, I gave our child away"?

Even imagining Allen's reaction was unbearable. The pain of the last twenty years was guilt enough. All she had were the first three days of the child's life: a beaded name band from the delivery room, a vague recollection of black hair and a newborn's blue eyes. And an ache inside herself, volcanic in proportion.

Those months of pregnancy had been shameful ones, borne alone for fear of telling her mother that she was pregnant. Once the secret could be hidden no longer, she had been marched off to the family doctor, and then her shame became her mother's. Maureen had just worked up the courage to write to Allen to tell him she was carrying his child when that awful news came that he had drowned in the waters off Cyprus.

Until then Allen's letters had been filled with glowing accounts of the beauty of Cyprus. The myths that intrigued him. The people that welcomed him when he went ashore. The heat of the Mediterranean and the blue of the sea. The cliffs, the enchantment of the sunsets. He had not written of the animosity between the Greeks and the Turks living there, but only of his fascination with the land of his mother's people, and thus his own land. Twice he had complained that the military restricted his exploration of the island, and twice he had written that he could hear the ringing of the ancient bells from the deck of his ship.

For days she visualized the blueness of Allen's watery grave. The calm waters that had claimed him. Thinking of it now, she was convinced that it would be better if she had never known Allen was alive. Seeing him again, sensing his nearness, had only awakened that deep longing to belong to him.

Why did you go away? he had asked.

She barely remembered the move from the coast up to Running Springs. Her brothers rebelled at being pulled out of their schools and away from their friends. No one seemed to care that she had left *her* friends behind as well.

"Blame it on your sister," her mother had said.

Paul and Robert resented her, and the more pregnant she became, the greater their displeasure. But seven-year-old Jason had remained her buddy. When the baby began to kick inside her, Jason had wanted to put his hand against her abdomen and feel the baby move.

Once he had asked, "Why is Mommy so angry at you?"

"Because I'm going to have a baby."

"Oh, I know that, but how did the baby get there?"

She had hugged him and said simply, "It is Allen's baby."

As she became more lumbering in her movements, and more fretful as the time for delivery neared, Jason had drawn away from her, convinced by his brothers that a baby "out of wedlock" was a disgrace to the family name. And so her mother had accomplished her goal—isolation and rejection.

Her mother arranged for the baby to be born in a Riverside hospital, but as the time neared, Maureen had thumbed a ride down the mountain from Running Springs and caught a bus into Newport. For two days she roamed the beach and slept in a shelter for homeless women. When her contractions began and her water broke, she spent her last few dollars on a taxi to the hospital, and presented herself in the emergency room.

It was too late to turn her away. She was already dilated five centimeters. The emergency room doctor who'd examined her shouted his orders. "This baby won't wait. Notify this kid's mother and admit her."

And so Meggy made her appearance in the well-scrubbed delivery room in the county where Maureen had met Allen. Maureen's low-grade fever kept them there for three days. Maureen cradled Meggy several times, fed her once each day, wept when they took her from the room. And argued with her mother.

"You can't keep the baby, Maureen."

"I won't give her up."

"You are very young, dear. You have your whole life ahead of you. The baby deserves a better chance than you can give her."

"Have you *seen* her, Mother? She's *mine.*"

She still remembered the brief flicker of sadness that crossed her mother's face. "Yes. She's very beautiful, Maureen. As pretty as you were when you were born."

"I want to call her Megan."

"Don't name her, Maureen. It only makes it more difficult." She had brushed the wrinkles from the spread on Maureen's bed. "I have someone I want you to talk to. A social worker."

In the end, Maureen signed the papers, and the nurse took the baby from her arms for the last time and walked out of the room.

She still remembered looking out the window of her hospital room toward the vast Pacific Ocean, as deep as her pain, and then looking down on the social worker leaving by the back exit of the hospital with an infant girl in her arms. She was a stern-looking woman carrying an extraordinary little girl who had been born as Baby Birkland and left with a new name and new identity. Tears had streamed down Maureen's cheeks as the car took the winding curve and disappeared from sight.

Slowly she had turned and dressed, putting on the clothes that her mother had spread out on the bed, and left the hospital with her arms empty, her heart aching.

"It's best," her mother had insisted. "They'll find a good home for the baby."

As they walked through the main door, she had felt faint. Her mother grabbed her arm, shaking her. "You're all right, Maureen? Should I get the nurse?"

She had despised Ellen Birkland in that moment, but she said, "All I want is my baby."

Maureen was left to grieve alone and to endure the second move in six months from Running Springs back to Cedar Lake. Young Jason never forgave her for not seeing the baby. Maureen never forgave herself for letting the baby go— Her front door bell rang. Startled from her ruminations, she made her way to answer it and was even more surprised to see Dwayne Crocker standing there with a pizza box in one hand, an attaché case in the other.

He gave her his affable grin. "Hi."

"Dwayne, who let you in downstairs?" He shrugged as she finger-combed her hair and stepped back. "Come in anyway."

"Been worried about you. Thought you might be sick."

"Then why did you bring pizza?"

"I'm hungry." He held up the briefcase. "Besides, I wanted to talk about the missile project."

"Couldn't it wait until tomorrow?"

"Thought you'd like a preview. Colonel Spencer is flying in from the Pentagon in the morning."

"Roland Spencer. Why?"

"To discuss more military contracts."

"That's Larhaven's business now."

"No, it's business as usual at Fabian until all the paperwork is in. Whichever way it goes, we're still going to get a big hunk of the defense and space contracts."

"You are sure of your job, Dwayne. But I'm on my way out."

"Hard to believe the way you're shining up to Allen Kladis."

"What's that supposed to mean?"

In his usual easygoing manner, he replied, "He's stepping on my territory. I don't like strangers coming in from the outside. I saw you cut out of the conference Wednesday, and Allen made a beeline for you. It didn't make McCormick feel happy when we saw you having lunch with Kladis. McCormick sees him as the enemy."

She felt sorry for Eddie, but said, "My business, Dwayne."

"I know, but I was just beginning to enjoy your company."

"After one dinner out?"

"I figured on more—until I drove by your condo yesterday. I came by to offer you a ride to work—and ask you out for dinner afterward." He gave his silver-rimmed glasses a shove back in place. "Look, I wasn't spying. I'd just parked and then I saw Kladis taking your steps two at a time. I got the picture real fast."

She snatched the pizza box from his hands and led the way into her immaculate white kitchen. "We'd better eat before it gets cold. Soda?" she asked, taking down plates and glasses.

"Coffee, if you don't mind."

She had calmed by the time they settled at the table. She poured his coffee as Dwayne cut generous portions of pizza for both of them.

"Dwayne, you must know there's nothing between us."

"You and Allen Kladis?"

"I was referring to you and me, Dwayne. We're colleagues, friends. Nothing more."

"Let me go on hoping." He looked up, his gaze piercing. "You need a good friend, don't you? And I'm your man."

"You're sweet. You know that, don't you?"

"I'm worried. I just don't want Kladis to let you down."

"Why would you think that?"

"He's moving in too fast."

Don't worry, she wanted to say, he's gone. Out of my life for the second time.

"You look wiped out, Maureen."

Not tired, she thought. *Lonely*. But it will never work out with Allen—nor with you, friend. Nor, probably, with the daughter out there somewhere who may not even know I'm alive.

Not just lonely, she corrected silently. *Heartbroken*.

Her voice sounded strained. "I have too much on my plate."

"And you don't mean pizza." He had already chowed down one piece and was cutting a second. "It looks more like there's too much on your mind. Okay, okay, I'll back off. But I'm only a phone call away if you need me. I know it's tough to get pushed out in the merger, but Colonel Spencer told me to tell you that if your job folds here, he has a place for you at the Pentagon. Guaranteed."

"He told me that before."

"Then it must be a sure thing."

He pushed back his empty plate, wiped the table dry with his shirt sleeve, and opened his briefcase. "I've been doing a lot of calculations, Maureen. I'm positive I have the Fabian missile snafu worked out."

His eyes sparkled as he pushed the paper toward her. "Now the way I see it..."

She leaned forward, grateful to get down to business. Somehow in his enthusiasm about missiles, Dwayne wasn't boring at all.

Sitting in the copilot seat, Allen watched with pride as his brother taxied out to the runway and then idled, waiting for clearance from the tower. Gray clouds lay to the left of the field, but they were not enough to deter Chris. "Seattle weather," he called it. "Wait for a cloudless blue sky and I'd never fly."

He was listening again and then he gave Allen a quick grin and a thumbs-up. "We're cleared for takeoff. Ready, big brother?"

"Ready. Let's go."

Now the sun was in their favor, breaking through the clouds. Chris revved the engine, and seconds later they whistled down the runway, building speed and then soaring like a bird skyward. Chris let their climbing speed increase and then he leveled the nose. Watching the excitement on Chris's face, Allen knew that his brother was totally at home in the air.

This was Chris's new dream machine: white as a swan, with dark blue stripes on the exterior and razor-thin wings almost blinding in the hazy glare of the sun. Chris had been logging up hours since he was sixteen, and sitting here with him, Allen realized that this was where his brother belonged—not cooped up in executive row. Chris was free-spirited, at home in the sky and miserable in a suit and tie.

"Chris, what would you think of piloting our company jet on a full-time basis between Larhaven and our plant in the south?"

"You keep me pretty busy on the ground."

"What if I lightened up? Put someone else in your office."

"You're serious?"

"Do you have a better idea?"

Chris urged the plane higher. "You used to talk about me logging up enough hours to be a test pilot for Larhaven."

"You don't have the military background."

"Maybe not. But I've been looking into it."

"Could you put it in writing? Then we'll submit it to the board. And don't worry about Nick's objections."

"Once the Fabian-Larhaven merger goes through, Allen, what are your plans?"

"Four or five years down the line, I'd like to retire."

"You can't let Nick take over Larhaven."

"I'd stay on to chair the Board. And keep my control on the stock. But now that I see you up here, Chris, doing what you want to do, it makes me rethink my goals."

Allen relaxed against the blue leather seat; he glanced around the cockpit and then at the familiar landmarks beneath them. "Beautiful," he said as they flew out over Puget Sound.

"The scenery, or the girl you left behind?"

"What?"

"Nick tells me you have a girl down in California. Says it's the girl you knew years ago."

"She's not a girl any longer."

"Is that good or bad?"

"She's lovely. It was like stepping back in time. She was married. Widowed now. There's a kid—a teenager, actually." Allen frowned. "But I didn't meet her. Maureen doesn't talk about her, either. I'm not sure what's going on."

"So are you taking this Maureen seriously or not?"

"I'm not certain what's going to happen, Chris. One minute it looks like things might progress, and then she pulls away."

"Do you like her?"

"I did twenty years ago."

"And now?"

"I'm sifting through my feelings. Trying not to rush things. I don't want to catch her on the rebound just because I'm lonely."

"It's been a year since Adrian," Chris said thoughtfully.

They were flying inland now; the Lake Washington Bridge lay below. Later as they flew over Snoqualmie Falls, Chris was saying, "Up here you can't help but feel that God is really out there somewhere."

Allen glanced at his brother and saw the strength in Chris's profile, the familial set of his jaw, the broad forehead, the sun-streaked brown hair. "That sounds odd coming from you, Chris."

"Not so crazy. Our grandmother was always into praying and talking about going to heaven on the angels' wings."

"So was our dad."

"The difference was our grandmother's talk was genuine."

"That's why I quoted her when Adrian was dying. Even told Adrian she would be borne on the wings of angels to heaven."

Chris gave him a crooked grin. "When my time comes, I'd like to check out that way. Hope Grams had the facts straight."

Allen looked away until Chris nudged him. "You've come a long journey, Allen. And Dad dumped a big job in your lap to run Larhaven. Don't let it hold you back. I have a feeling you're searching for something. If it's not the girl in California—"

What else could it be? wondered Allen, but he cut Chris off. "I had no idea she was there. What makes me sick is that the merger will cost Maureen her job."

"That doesn't exactly make for good relationships.... Hey, wait a minute. You're not suggesting my flying for the company so you can find a spot for this Maureen?"

"She's a research scientist—into missiles."

"Then she wouldn't want my job in finance. Look, Allen, why don't you talk to our sister-in-law? She's good about things of the heart."

"Fran?"

"Yeah, tell her about Maureen."

"Nick probably gave her an earful already."

"Now you can tell Fran the truth. Besides, Fran's been wanting to match you up with someone for a long time."

They were flying west again, back toward the airport. "Fran is a bit like our grandmother, don't you think? She'd lend a kind ear to discussing this Maureen of yours. And she's into praying."

Chris was checking in with the tower again, preparing for the final approach. As his brother lined up with the runway, Allen glanced out the cockpit window again. This was his kid brother, confident, and a wise old bird, too, young as he was—smart about people and the ways of the heart. Allen had never felt so proud of him, never felt so close to him. How had Chris read him so thoroughly, pierced him so deeply? What else did he know about the *girl* in California?

Chapter Twelve

It was a clear, crisp June morning, and a good day for Maureen to be making her first flight to the northwest. She had grabbed at Eddie McCormick's assignment to catch the 6:45 a.m. plane to Seattle, with a quick forty-eight-hour turnaround on the red-eye flight back to Orange County. She agreed to take scrupulous notes on the operational system at Larhaven and come back prepared to guide them all in the transfer to Larhaven policy.

She was traveling light as she always did on business trips, with a carry-on in the overhead and her trench coat hanging in the first-class closet—crushed and wrinkled, no doubt. She had no baggage claim check to worry about when she reached SeaTac. But now as she rode alone in the spaciousness of first-class, with the barren bulkhead in front of her, she was having second thoughts. Dwayne Crocker was better suited to the task. He would have gone without any emotional conflict.

Almost a month had gone by since Allen had returned to Seattle. Since then she had not heard from him directly. No phone calls nor letters, and no certified letter from Larhaven advising her that her services were no longer needed. Dared she hope? No, none of the team had received the severance notice.

The only word from Allen had been his routine memos to the management team at Fabian; those related to the missile projects had been faxed directly to her office; confidential details arrived in a sealed pouch. Once Allen had added a quick "hi" in the corner and ended his note, writing, *It was good to see you on my trip south. Trust you and your daughter are doing well.*

Maybe he could put aside their time together without a second thought. She could not. A business trip? Who was she fooling? She was flying to the northwest to see Allen again and she knew it—like some infatuated teenager.

A battle line formed in her mind. Right brain. Left brain. A raging battle between her practical self and the sensitive emotional part of her that could not forget Allen Kladis. As well, she was fighting for her own position in southern California when the merger went through. As long as the dreaded certified letter had not arrived, there was still a chance.

Maureen crossed her legs, and too late realized that her coffee cup had spilled, leaving it half empty. She beckoned for the flight attendant to take her tray away, but snatched up the colorful piece of paper that had arrived with her breakfast. A greeting from the airline.

An odd place, she thought, to find a Psalm of praise that told her to be thankful. *Give thanks,* it said. Give thanks? she wondered, when I'm in love with someone who does not love me back—a man who is grieving for someone else? Give thanks when my job security may be swept away? Give thanks when I don't even know whether my only child is alive, or, if so, whether she knows I exist?

She mused over the words as she leaned back to enjoy the view out her window. In the distance, rivulets of clouds hovered above the mountains of northern California. Their peaks were snowcapped, their lava-ridged slopes scarred with deep eroded crevices. The mountain range looked like foothills from 35,000 feet, the wide blanket of clouds like a king-size eiderdown quilt.

For years Maureen had played the game of respectability—attending a large, popular church and yet never knowing peace with God. Being accepting of the flaws she saw in others, yet never forgiving herself for the blunders of her youth. She was a frequent speaker at business conferences talking about "The Successful Woman in the Corporate Workplace." Speaking at conferences was something she enjoyed thoroughly, and did with efficiency and humor, yet never speaking her heart, never revealing things that really mattered to her.

She closed her eyes. When she opened them again fifteen minutes later, the plane was caught in turbulence, bouncing up and down with the luggage juggling wildly in the overhead. As the plane shuddered, the pilot said calmly, "Ladies and gentlemen, please fasten your seat belts."

Maureen peered out the window. The ridged pattern of gray clouds looked more like the gutted tracks of a wagon wheel marking a trail across the sky. The distant horizon was faint like a morning mist. They were well into Oregon now, the plane outdistancing the turbulence as it moved effortlessly toward the Washington border. SeaTac lay ahead. Then Seattle, Larhaven Aircraft—and Allen. There was no turning back.

* * *

Maureen drove up to the gate at Larhaven and identified herself. She was given a visitor's pass and directed to the visitors' parking lot. Moments later she was inside the main building, the sound of her high heels mellowed by the thick carpets.

A pretty receptionist greeted her warmly. "Oh, Mrs. Davenport. Yes, we're expecting you."

She dialed and said, "Mr. Kladis, Mrs. Davenport is here.... Yes, I'll tell her."

She flashed her gracious smile again. "Mr. Kladis will be here in a minute."

Maureen glanced around as she waited, trying to still the wild thumping of her heart, and wondering whether Allen would come from a rear corridor, or appear at the head of the stairwell, or arrive by way of the elevator on the far side of the building. The lobby was spacious, efficient, no expense spared.

She turned quickly as the elevator door opened. Nick Kladis stepped out and strolled confidently toward her, a younger, good-looking man at his side. *Allen is not coming,* she thought.

"Mrs. Davenport," Nick boomed, taking her hand and pumping it. "No trouble finding us?"

"Not at all," she replied smoothly. But she was working hard to hide her disappointment.

Allen. Where was Allen?

Nick kept holding her hand, causing the receptionist to peer around the flower vase to eye them quizzically. "The CEO is unable to be with you this morning, Mrs. Davenport," Nick said.

Allen doesn't want to see me again, she thought bitterly. But why the formality, as though they had never been on a first-name basis? Why not Allen, or my brother—not the CEO, as though he were a stranger?

"So what's his schedule, Nick?" she asked. "Eddie McCormick was expecting me to spend the day with your CEO."

Nick's eyes narrowed. "He has his usual Monday morning board meeting. And then some last-minute things to go over with the lawyers." Nick beamed slyly, placating her. "It will be good to have the merger settled, don't you think?"

"We're trying to cooperate. That's why Eddie McCormick sent me here. To learn what I could."

"We thought that odd." He laughed harshly. "What do you expect to accomplish in a day or two? Or are you trying to take over Larhaven...my job perhaps?"

He turned to the man beside him. "Chris, this is Mrs. Davenport, the research scientist from Fabian."

Not one of the "vice-presidents," she noted.

"I'm the youngest Kladis," Chris said pleasantly. "The nicest of the lot."

Nick scowled at both of them. "I've arranged for Chris to work with you today and tomorrow. He'll give you a tour of the plant. He knows our operational system from *A* to *Z.* Anything you need to know, ask him."

Unlike his brothers, Chris was fair-haired, shorter, calm; his eyes were more hazel than brown. "We'll work out of my office," he told her, then flashed a charming smile. "It's less stuffy than executive row."

She liked Chris immediately. His smile was genuine and friendly. But something was passing between the brothers that was neither civil nor cordial.

"Time to get back to my stuffy office...and do some real work," Nick said.

Chris took his brother's retort without rancor. "We'd better get started, Mrs. Davenport."

"Maureen, please."

"Suits me. I'm not much for all this formality. We'll tour the plant first."

"She'll need clearance," Nick reminded Chris.

"Allen took care of that. Here." He produced another badge. "Security clearance for the day." He picked up her overnighter and briefcase. "This way, Maureen."

"I'll drop by from time to time," Nick said. "And the CEO—"

"Allen?" she added.

"Yes. Allen said he has a business lunch to attend. He'll try to see you by supper time. Depends on how his day goes."

"Depends on how you scheduled his day, Nick," Chris said.

"That being the case, I'm certain he'll be tied up." She glanced at Chris and sent him a radiant smile. "I'm ready."

He arched one brow playfully. "I've never met anyone who was ready for a day with the Kladis brothers."

"Try me."

"Gladly," he said as he led her toward the elevator.

Chris's corner office was simple, spartan, located in a corridor away from the main Larhaven offices. Maureen wondered if it was Chris's choice or the family reminder that he was not "top dog" at Larhaven. But Chris didn't seem to mind. It was as though the youngest brother had been cut from a kindlier mold.

The tour of the plant was incredible and far more elaborate than Fabian. When they reached the final assembly line where the planes were readied for flight, he touched the nose of one of the military aircraft as gently as he would have stroked a kitten.

"I'd like to test fly one of these babies, but the best I can hope for right now is commercial flying."

"Do you have your license?"

"I will when I get in enough hours. And then I'd like to go on to be a test pilot."

"Is there a chance?"

"Allen thinks so. Nick opposes it."

"If that doesn't work out, do you say goodbye to Larhaven?"

"I would have done that long ago if it hadn't been for Allen. I had my resignation written out when Adrian got sick. We brothers may not get on, but we are loyal."

"You're married?"

"No, I'm the bachelor." He studied her seriously, his gaze approving. "If I met someone like you, I'd marry. There are girls here at Larhaven, but I'm not interested. And when I'm not working, I'm flying. Or off camping. Or servicing my plane out at Orange County."

"Maybe you'll meet up with a female mechanic someday."

"There is one—but she's not happy with me right now because I spent the last two weekends camping with my brother."

"That's right. Allen told me you were going into Canada."

"We did—finally. He was like a new man. Been coming around ever since that trip to California. That's another reason I haven't quit. Allen still needs me—until he finds the right girl again. And then I'm out of here."

"I wouldn't wait that long."

He flipped open another operational ledger. His next comment caught her off guard. "You were disappointed when he didn't meet you in the lobby this morning."

She blushed. "Did it show that much?"

"Don't worry. Your secret's safe with me."

They had lunch in the plant cafeteria and then went

back to work. Nick dropped in two or three times during the afternoon, staying long enough to scan her notes and then disappearing as quickly as he had come. But Allen never showed up.

"Nick's like that," Chris said as he left the room for the third time. "Always checking up on you. I think it's his safeguard so no one will think to question his activities. We were at each other's throats this morning."

"Why?"

"Over you, Mrs. Davenport. He thinks you're after his job."

"What? He was serious when he said that?"

"He's always wary of intelligent women. I told him that he needed to warn you that you're still on Allen's expendable list down there at Fabian. Did he?"

"I thought the list was predetermined, Chris. But I still don't have any official notice."

"Allen vacillates, especially where you're concerned. Then he and Nick have a go-round on it."

"Why are you telling me all of this, Chris?"

"Because I like you...and because my family gave you the shaft twenty years ago."

Her head shot back, and she pushed the hair from her face. "So you know about that?"

"It was the dinner conversation when I was a kid."

"And not very pleasant to listen to, I imagine. What about now?"

"Nick keeps bringing it up. I think he's worried about you and Allen really making a go of it."

"Nick can stop worrying. Allen hasn't called me since leaving California. And right now, he's avoiding me."

"If there's anything I can do to help you, Maureen..."

"Chris, I don't need favors."

"But you need a job, Maureen. Do you have another one lined up after the merger?"

"I've some leads, but no real offers," she admitted.

"I could put in a good word for you. As long as you don't cross Allen, he may put someone else on the expendable list."

"That doesn't sound like Allen. He was always fair. And, Chris, I wouldn't want anyone at Fabian to lose his job on my account. The others are family men. I just have myself to care for. You understand, don't you, Chris?"

"Just yourself?" He seemed surprised, but she couldn't fathom why. Across the desk, their eyes met. "Allen is a good man, Maureen. But he tries to keep Larhaven and his private life separate. It's killing him."

She was exhausted by closing time. It had been a long day going over the operational procedures, but she had taken copious notes and would be able to implement them at Fabian. "You've been a brick, Chris. Thanks for putting up with me all day."

"It's just good business," he teased as she locked her attaché case. "I'm counting on spending tomorrow with you, too."

"I don't think so, Chris. I'm anxious to get back home. If we've missed anything major, you can fax or call me."

"You should stay two or three days to get a real feel for our policies.... You're not running, are you, Maureen?"

She felt her neck grow warm and busied herself checking her watch. "McCormick insisted on a quick turnaround. He'd like twenty-four hours better than forty-eight. I'm certain I can get a flight out tonight."

"It's Allen, isn't it?" Chris asked. "His not showing up."

"It's okay. You made it okay."

He smiled. "What about dinner, Maureen? Nick's wife said we could join them, but that's a madhouse. What about the Space Needle? We can browse out there until it's time for your plane."

"Oh, Chris, I can't take any more of your day."

From behind her, a deep voice said, "And I definitely don't want him spending any more time with you."

She spun around, startled. Allen was striding into the room, his arms extended, his eyes bright with welcome. She caught the heady scent of his cologne as he hugged her, felt the warmth of his strong arms around her.

She drew back, breathless. "I guess your day was full?"

"Too full—thanks to all those meetings Nick arranged. Oh, Maureen, I was afraid I'd miss you."

She saw Chris grinning. "See you," he mouthed, and left them.

"Did Chris give you the grand tour? Answer all your questions?"

"He did." She was flustered. "He was great. I like him."

"He's the wrong Kladis brother for you."

Her pulse raced. "Is there a right one?"

"I keep hoping. Look, my meetings are done for the day. Let's just get out of here. Say, to dinner and out for the evening?"

"There's been a change of plans. I'm leaving tonight."

He frowned. "But I thought you were here for two days."

"Chris piled everything into one day."

His frown deepened. "We can still have dinner, then I'll take you to the airport. But let's run out to my condo first."

She hesitated. "Why the condo?"

"So you can see where I live. So I can change." He tipped her chin up. "It's all right, Maureen. We won't talk about Adrian. Agreed?"

"Agreed," she said. But she'll be there, Maureen thought. As real as if she were still alive.

Chapter Thirteen

Allen opened the door and let Maureen step into the condo ahead of him. "Have a look about."

He held up his attaché case, grinning. "I'll just put my things away and change. We'll have plenty of time for dinner before driving to SeaTac." He nodded toward the wall clock. "You won't have to check in until after eleven. I could cook something up here," he offered. "I'm good at charbroiled steaks and tossed salads."

She didn't want to sit at Adrian's table, in Adrian's chair. "Let's go out. Do you mind?"

"Not at all."

As Allen disappeared into his bedroom, Maureen looked around the living room, with its white brick fireplace on one side, and logs set to burn. Her attention was immediately drawn to the wedding photo on the mantel.

Kicking Allen's worn slippers beneath the end table, she cleared a path for herself. En route, she picked up the business magazines that had been tossed on the floor between Allen's easy chair and the smaller matching one where Adrian must have sat beside him. When she reached the mantel, she took the wedding photo up in both hands and studied Adrian's lovely face. Blue eyes, she noted, full of trust and love as she looked up at her bridegroom.

It was Maureen's first real glimpse of the woman that Allen had married, and an overwhelming sense of loss gripped her.

That should have been *me,* she thought.

Maureen set the photo down, and, with remorse, drew back. She was still gazing at the picture when Allen came back into the room. "Your wife was beautiful," she said, turning to face him.

At the mention of his wife, the shadows returned to his dark eyes. "She was. But I thought we agreed, we wouldn't speak of Adrian—not this evening."

He had slipped into his casual clothes, khaki slacks and a polo shirt that fit tightly across his broad chest and muscular arms. His hands were filled—two goblets of sparkling cider on a tray with raw vegetables and oyster crackers.

Her hand brushed his as she rescued the tray, sending an electric shock wave through her body. Old feelings for Allen swept over her again as she put the tray on the coffee table and lifted a goblet to her lips.

"Shall we sit in here?" he asked, popping a cracker in his mouth.

She glanced casually at Adrian's chair. "It's too warm."

"You're right." He snatched up one of the glasses and quenched his thirst with a quick swallow. Then he held out his hand. She took it. "Come, let's sit on the veranda, Maureen."

He led her through the master bedroom, apologizing

for the clutter. "I'm not neat as a pin—the way you were, Reeny."

Reeny! The old nickname had slipped in again unintended. He released her hand and pushed back the sliding glass door.

Her breath caught as they stepped out on the veranda. "What a marvelous view."

"That's Lake Washington. I sail there whenever I can. And that tower over there—that's the university." He pointed with his glass, spilling a few drops on the porch. "Did so well in my undergraduate work that I took my Master's there, too." The serious lines around his mouth and eyes relaxed. "Dad was footing the bill, grooming me for the big takeover."

"He groomed you well." She sat down, the warmth of the sun and the heat of her emotions bringing a flush to her cheeks.

"Reeny, I wasn't referring to the merger of our companies."

"It's all right. Expansion was what your father dreamed about all along."

"How would you know that?"

"From Nick. Unlike you, he's quite talkative. I rather think he would like your job, Allen." For a split second she hesitated. "And if your position is not up for grabs, then Chris thinks Nick would settle for mine, as head of the missile program."

Allen faced the railing now, his goblet balanced on the ledge, his back to her. The afternoon breeze made jagged ends of his dark hair. "Nick has been talking out of turn."

"Aren't you still planning to eliminate the top five positions at Fabian? Mine included?"

As he turned, the fading sun filtered through the trees

and caught the glint of silver at his temples; a new worry line had wedged between his brows. "The Larhaven Board has discussed it. It will save millions with all of the stock privileges and benefit buybacks that your people have."

"Allen, do you plan any other cutbacks?"

He seemed to stiffen. "Among the rank and file? Not for several months. But once we streamline the system, many positions will be eliminated. You know that's how mergers go. Cutbacks are inevitable."

Why, Allen? Why me? she wondered. Are you punishing me for twenty years ago? Does my presence here threaten to sully your memories of a perfect marriage to Adrian? No, Allen for all of his calculated business moves was not a vengeful man.

Her anger flared. "But why *my* job, Allen?"

"I've told you. Eliminating the top positions saves money. I didn't know it would affect you, not when that decision was made. I wish I could work out a job for you up here."

"I live in California."

"But if you'd be willing to relocate—"

"What *kind* of a job, Allen? Something you have to create? I'm a research scientist."

"A capable one, according to Eddie McCormick."

"Are you trying to buy me off?"

"That's unfair, Reeny."

The memory of Alexander Kladis suddenly thrust itself on her. She could still recall Allen's father spreading the ten thousand-dollar bills out on the table with meticulous care. "You must never see my son again, Miss Birkland. You do understand?"

She had recoiled. Mr. Kladis was trying to buy her

with tainted money, to control her destiny as he did his sons.

Quickly her mother had promised, "My daughter will cooperate."

"No, I won't, Mother. I won't let him bribe me."

Kladis had stood abruptly and cocked the brim of his Scottish cap over one eye. He was a determined man, strong and confident like Allen, his eyes dark and threatening. He had a sharp mind. A sharp tongue.

Maureen had been three months' pregnant, her pregnancy known by no one but herself. Allen had promised to come back to her in the summer. She grabbed the money and flung it at Allen's father. "You could never pay me enough money to stay away from your son."

Two months later Alexander Kladis came back. The Birkland living room had been reduced to packing crates and suitcases in preparation for the move to Running Springs. Maureen was on the second floor, leaning over the balcony, forbidden to come down—her pregnancy evident now. Mr. Kladis had glanced up and guessed the truth. On that second visit he had counted out the ten one-thousand-dollar bills into Ellen Birkland's hand. "That should cover your daughter's expenses," he said.

Her mother had curled her fingers around the money. "I will see that she gets it. Now get out, Mr. Kladis, and never come back. Your family has caused us enough grief already."

Allen's voice drew her back from the memories. "Reeny, I want to find a job for you here, but the board opposes bringing anyone new into our missile program."

"Especially a woman?"

She knew she had nailed him. She saw the pulsating tic that ran along his jaw. "The men on the board of directors are of the same mind. Several of them were here when Dad was in power."

"No women on the board? What happened to equal opportunities?"

"We've had women. They usually don't last out their term."

"Then try me," she said defiantly. "I've stood up to senators and congressmen before and I won't back down."

Allen looked miserable as he blew on the edge of his glass and watched the tiny bubbles drip down the sides of the goblet. "I have my brothers to contend with."

"Surely Chris isn't a problem?"

"In spite of Nick's arguments, I can offer you a substantial severance arrangement. I'll hold out for enough funds to cover three months of living while you find another job."

"How long are you going to stay at a job that you find so distasteful?" she asked bluntly.

His neck snapped as he turned toward her. "Long enough to make certain that Nick is ready to take over— that he won't waste company funds or make foolish moves that would destroy the company. Dad worked hard to build Larhaven."

"And Alexander Kladis picked his board and management team with great care. I suppose you control them in the same way, with long- and short-term incentive plans, stock options, and a satisfactory severance that makes retirement worthwhile if you want someone out of the company?"

Allen's neck went crimson. "You don't understand," he said soberly. "There have to be cutbacks."

"Oh, I do understand. You've changed. You're like your—"

"Like my father?" He spat the words out. "I promised my mother—and my grandmother before her—that I would stick with this company until it was a place of integrity like it was when my father started here from scratch."

His rage was audible. "My father was good man in the beginning, Reeny. He was smart. Industrious. Willing to take gambles. He succeeded, but it destroyed our family life. Mother would have given anything to call it quits and go back to Cyprus—but she loved him, and tolerated his greed."

"Must the Kladis brothers carry on the father's traditions?"

His gaze wandered, but his voice remained steady. "We have a large chunk of the commercial market—and I take family pride in that. We'll continue the military contracts here and at Fabian and build on them. But in another five years, most of Dad's friends—the worst of his cronies—will be out of here. Retired."

"With a substantial pension that will cover a mansion and a yacht, while hundreds of employees at Fabian will have lost their jobs by then. The little guys take the fall for any merger. Think about it, Allen. Pink slips in their mailboxes won't pay the bills or feed the children."

"Reeny, don't expect me to run this company on emotions. I keep the cost basis in the forefront. And it's my responsibility to arrange financial backing for the mid-west takeover within the next few months."

"More expansions? When will it stop, Allen? When will you stop burying yourself in this job and go back to living life and loving it?"

"When I find someone to love, who will live life with me." He jammed his hands in his pockets. "Whatever it takes, I'm going to make this a company with men and women of integrity at the helm. With Dad's friends gone, the voting in our meetings will change."

"Why don't you fire them?"

"It's out of my hands. Dad repaid their loyalties with job security. Given my five-year goal—and if Fran's influence counts for anything—Nick may be ready to assume a real place of leadership. Perhaps he's not the man I'd prefer to take over," he added honestly, "but he's my brother and it's time I step down."

"You're not really happy here, are you?"

For a long moment he looked at her. "I could be.... I thought life was over when I lost Adrian. When I lost you, I could let you go because I thought you had walked out on me. But I had no *choice* where my wife was concerned," he said bitterly.

She ached for him now—seeing Adrian not as competition, but as Allen's deep loss. Gently, she said, "You can still choose to let Adrian go. You have to go on with your own life, Allen. Find someone. Settle down again. Love. Be loved."

His eyes filled with longing. "I thought I *had* found someone." With obvious mounting despair, he ran his hand through his hair. "Oh, Reeny, I never meant to hurt you."

She wanted to believe him. But why had he brought her to the condo? To prove to both of them that Adrian was his one true love? She had to lash back and hurt him as he was hurting her—by thrusting Adrian in her face, by destroying her career. But she couldn't leave without telling Allen the truth.

His somber dark eyes looked straight through her. "Why can't we pick up as though it were yesterday? A month ago when you walked into that conference room, it was as though those twenty years were erased. For a few days I was certain you felt the same way. Why can't we go on from here?''

"Because it's not the same, Allen," she murmured. "Because there's something you don't know."

She had his attention. "Allen," she blurted, "do you remember me telling you about my daughter?"

"Yes, of course."

"But there's something I didn't tell you." She inhaled sharply, unable to hold back the truth any longer. "She's yours. She's your daughter, Allen."

The goblet in Allen's hand crashed to the patio porch and shattered into glistening shards. "What? What are you saying, Reeny?"

There was no turning back. "You have a child."

His face went rigid; his eyes darkened. "A child?"

"A daughter. She's almost twenty."

The pulse along Allen's jaw throbbed. "Meggy?" he asked.

"Yes. Meggy."

In the doorway behind them, someone whistled. "Nick," Allen said huskily, the color drained from his face. "He always appears at inopportune moments."

"Then I'd better go."

"No, I want to know more. I must know more about Meggy," he insisted.

And what will I tell you? she wondered. That I haven't seen her since she was born? That I deserted her the way you deserted me so long ago? "Some other time," she said.

Nick was on the veranda now, chewing a raw carrot stick, his fist full of oyster crackers. "Thanks for the snacks. Hey—did I walk in on something?"

"Don't you usually? If you'd only ring the bell—"

"Your door's always unlocked when you're home, big brother. I just thought—"

The blazing fury in Allen's eyes frightened Maureen. His lips barely parted as he said, "Look, Nick, whatever you need, we can talk about it later. Maureen and I are going out to dinner."

"No, dinner's out. I don't have the stomach for food." She put her empty glass down. "Don't bother, Allen. I'll let myself out. But may I use your phone first? I want to call a taxi."

His voice was stiff, toneless. "I told you I'd take you to SeaTac after we have dinner."

"I've lost my appetite." She leaned down and picked up her purse. "It's been a busy twenty-four hours."

"A shocking twenty-four hours," he countered.

"Allen, I'm going to try and catch an earlier flight back to California. I hate the red-eyes anyway."

Allen's expression remained stony, his dark eyes shiny with unshed tears. "We haven't finished the business at hand."

She smiled, the muscles of her face barely moving. "I think we said goodbye a long time ago."

Allen stood riveted to the porch, his back braced against the iron rails. She imagined him looking this distraught the day Adrian died, and she hated herself for hurting him again.

Frowning at his brother, Nick stepped to her side. "I'll drive you to SeaTac, Mrs. Davenport," he offered.

"Would you? My carry-on and raincoat are in Allen's trunk."

"No problem." He snatched up Allen's key chain from the table. "I can transfer them."

She glanced back toward the veranda. Allen was leaning into the railing now, his fists jammed into his pockets. "He seems to take great comfort standing there, Nick. The lake is beautiful."

"I rather think it's his memories of Adrian. They sailed out there every chance they had."

"Yes, he mentioned that," Maureen replied. Actually, he'd tactfully mentioned that *he* often sailed out there.

"But I can say this for him," Nick added, "thanks to you, he's determined to get past her death. He's doing better."

She nodded distractedly. Yes, Allen would find his way back to peace and contentment, no matter how long it took. But would he ever get over what she had just done to him?

"Will you be coming back here again, Mrs. Davenport?" he asked as he shut the front door.

"I don't think so. Chris said we can conduct business by phone and fax and e-mail. That should take care of my responsibility to your brother."

"Which one?" He touched her elbow and led her down the steps to the sidewalk. "Chris can handle life on his own. It's Allen who needs someone like you to bring him around. In spite of what my father said, you and Allen had something good once. Long before Adrian."

"That was twenty years ago," Maureen replied, surprised at Niko's sudden flash of kindness. Maybe he wasn't the cold cynic he pretended to be after all.

"It's not too late," he persisted.

But it *was* too late. She had just thrown Allen a curve ball from which he might never recover. "Nick, just drive me to SeaTac, and let *me* worry about my own future."

"Do you really have one without Allen?"

"I won't have a job at Larhaven, if that's what you mean. That's not why I came up here."

"I was thinking of something bigger."

Exasperated, she glared at him.

He winked. "Like I told you, Allen needs you."

"He has his memories."

"That's part of his past."

"So am I."

"No," Nick said, lighting a cigarette. "You could be part of his future, too. You need each other."

"I thought you couldn't stand me, Nick."

"I couldn't at first. I thought you were after Allen's money—or my job."

No, Allen's love, she thought.

"But my wife set me straight after talking to Chris this evening. Fran and Chris say you're genuine."

Tears burned behind her eyes. "They don't even know me."

"Go ahead and cry. It will do you good."

"It's your cigarette smoke that's getting to me."

"Sorry." He flicked the cigarette to the sidewalk and crushed it with his shoe. "There. Satisfied?"

He transferred her luggage to his own van and then held open the door for her. "Sure you won't change your mind?"

"It's too late," she repeated in a whisper.

Nick slid into the driver's seat beside her and turned the key. "I overheard what you told Allen back there. I'm sorry—but the truth is, I always knew there was a kid. Dad hired a private investigator. That's how we learned you left Orange County and moved to Running Springs."

"That—that old goat."

He smiled, amused. "I have better names for him.

Dad kept a file on you with notations about his trips to California to see you. After his second trip he wrote down that you were pregnant." He glanced her way. "To his credit, Dad felt some responsibility that it would be his grandchild. That's why he left the money."

"And not to buy me off?"

"That, too. But if you were pregnant, he thought the money would help." Allen sounded sulky. "I gave my old man five grandkids, but they were never enough. Even named the eldest one after him. But nothing I ever did was enough for my dad." He switched lanes, cutting back in too closely. "Allen was always the golden boy."

"He was the eldest son, Nick."

"Don't you think I *know* that? I've had it for breakfast, lunch and dinner all my life. Never could please that man. If Fran and I had produced a daughter, it would have been my ticket to success. Allen never wanted to be CEO. He did it to spite me."

"Allen is not like that, Nick."

"You just wait and see. Walking out on him like you just did, that termination letter will be on your desk by Monday."

Her spine stiffened. Maybe she didn't know Allen as well as she thought. Like father, like son?

"I thought you just said Allen and I had a future together."

"You would if you weren't both so stubborn." For a second he laid on the horn. Then, back in control, he said, "That money my dad gave you—he would have sent more, but then we heard that Allen was lost in Cyprus. As far as Dad was concerned, that just about guaranteed there'd be no paternity suit."

"Your father must have hated me."

"No. He just had plans for his eldest son. By the time

we knew that Allen was still alive, Dad couldn't locate you.''

"Did he try?''

"Mom insisted, but you had left Running Springs without leaving a forwarding address. Where did you go?''

"Indiana. And we did leave a forwarding address with the post office—good for a year. Did your dad really try?''

"The truth is, I don't know, Mrs. Davenport. Mother wanted Dad to send more money. But Alexander always did what he wanted.''

"If your folks knew, then Allen knew all along, didn't he? So why did he act so surprised when I told him about Meggy?''

"He didn't know about the baby. He didn't even know about Dad's file until I told him a few weeks ago. I've been dragging my heels about giving it to him. But now that he knows the truth, he will really want to meet his Meggy.''

"He can't, Nick.''

"Why not? Surely he has the right to see his own daughter. It's his kid, isn't it?''

She wanted to slap Nick as they veered through the traffic. "Yes, she's Allen's child.''

"Then arrange a meeting.''

"I can't, Nick. I don't even know Meggy's real name.... I gave her up for adoption when she was born.''

Chapter Fourteen

Three days later on a hot summer morning, Allen sat in his corporate office in the elaborately furnished room that had once been his father's, at the massive mahogany desk where his father had made his mark on the aircraft industry. A five-by-seven photo of Adrian sat in a silver frame looking up at him. He stared back at her, then picked up the photo and examined it.

Without her picture, the details of her lovely face and sparkling eyes would fade, the memories would slip away. Yet he looked at her now with less pain than he had six months ago. This time he did not wallow in self-pity, did not wish her back. Only a fool would call her back to those months of suffering and dying. He had no words for it. The poets did. She had *slipped the bounds of earth*.

He tried to picture her as smiling, laughing, well again, running free. But that gave her human form, and he knew enough to know that she had left that behind. But his grandmother's description of heaven, with glorious singing and streets of gold and a river of life, seemed out of reach to him. Impractical.

Let Adrian go, Maureen had said.

He put the picture down, angling it so the sun coming in through the windows caught the smile on Adrian's face. Shaking off his musings, he went back to the reports piled on his desk: the latest memos from Eddie McCormick at Fabian, the newest contract from Roland Spencer at the Pentagon and the initial legal documents from his board of directors for the planned takeover of the failing aircraft company in the mid-west. The balance sheets on the profit ledger were looking good; the mergers would make them look better. Nick had his problems, but his mind worked like a calculator. Nick kept his fingers on the balance sheet. He was good at his job but not prepared for running Larhaven.

Allen had seen little of Nick since that miserable encounter at the condo. He still resented Nick for walking in unannounced, and resented him even more for walking out of the house with Maureen. There had been messages left on his answering machine—calls from Nick, from Chris, and frantic calls from Fran, but he had ignored them all.

He had just circled a figure on the balance sheet when his door swung open and Nick charged in. Allen glared at him as he crossed the room, noticing a manila envelope clasped under his arm. Nick slapped the envelope on top of Allen's worksheets. Words in their father's familiar scrawl boldly marked the front: California. Important.

Allen knew, but he asked anyway, ''What's this, Nick?''

''Dad's file on Maureen.''

Unwinding the string, Allen extracted an age-worn

folder and read the typed label: Maureen Birkland. Allen wet his lips. "I have no use for this."

"I think you do. Don't judge the contents without reading them."

"Maureen's idea?" he asked as Nick walked away.

"You asked me to get the file for you a while back. Do what you want with it. And what you do with Maureen is your own business. But you gave her the shaft and that's not like you. If I'm to believe Chris, the fool woman is in love with you."

"In love with me! She gave me the jolt of my life. Is that love?"

"She didn't get pregnant on her own," Nick said. "Maybe it's about time you faced up to your own responsibility."

Allen gave a churlish laugh. "That coming from you?"

As the door closed behind Nick, Allen massaged his temples. Then he leaned forward and pressed the button on the intercom. "Vangie, hold my calls. If they're pressing, refer them to Nick."

"Yes, sir. Are you all right, Mr. Kladis?"

"All right," he said, knowing that everything was all wrong.

The folder contained two dozen investigative forms, barely legible, with a signature that looked like Sam Murdock, and a snapshot of the youthful Maureen caught on the run. Receipts for payments to Murdock's expenses and a withdrawal slip from his father's bank account for ten-thousand dollars were clipped together. His father's personal notations read like a journal. Allen poured over them, angered by the realization that his family—at least his dad, and, therefore, most likely his mother—knew about the birth of his daughter. At least they knew that Maureen was pregnant. The bitterness he felt at knowing that they had withheld the truth from him was unbearable.

August 8: We had a postcard from Allen today. The surfing is good. Ten days of nothing but surfing. I trust that he gets this frivolity out of his system. I have great plans for my son.

August 12: His mother tells me that Allen has met a girl on the beach in California. Sofia wants him to marry a nice girl from Cyprus. His third cousin, I believe. This is a foolish woman that I have married. My son will one day take a wife of wealth and position, not someone like his mother—as lovely as she is. I am grooming Allen for the aircraft industry. I will educate him for the position that he will one day fill.

September 20: Allen is not coming home. He tells us that he is in love. He is determined to marry this girl in California—this beautiful beach bum that he has met. She is only seventeen and still in high school. I will not let Allen ruin his life. I have hired a private investigator.

September 30: Allen refuses to take my calls. Our quarrel has reached into my home. Sofia and I are constantly battling about this matter. Nick tells us that he should be the one to take over the family business. But my confidence is in Allen.

October 1: The private investigator has sent us a picture of this Maureen Birkland taken as she passed him on the street. Even so we can see that she is a pretty girl. But very young.

October 12: The investigator lost Allen and the girl on the mountain road to Big Bear when his car spun out in a light snowfall. I have terminated his contract and replaced him.

October 30: Sofia tells me that my fury at the girl is out of control. I tell her to hush, to tend her own business. She cannot understand how much I have planned for my son's future.

November 15: I grieve that my son has joined the navy. That girl has ruined his life. But Allen tells me that once his girl graduates from high school— once she turns eighteen and he gets his first leave— that they will marry. He will not be coming home again. Ever. Unless we accept her.

December 31: The wedding is off! The navy has shipped my son off on a peacekeeping mission. My wife is such a foolish woman. She is proud of the snapshot of her son in uniform. She is telling everyone that he is on board a ship off the coast of Cyprus. She is certain that he will meet the nice Greek girl now—her third cousin. Sofia tells me, "Be happy, Alexander, our son will not marry the girl from California."

Be happy with my son in the navy—with my plans shelved?

Allen felt rage at his father as he read the January 5th notation: I must find this Maureen Birkland and pay her well so she will not wait for my son. I am certain the girl can be bought with ten-thousand dollars. With even less, perhaps.

For a moment Allen could not go on. He felt betrayed. He massaged the back of his neck, but the miserable headache refused to go away. Is that what happened, Reeny? he wondered. My father bought you with his money? No wonder you went away.

He started to shove the journal away and then, enraged, read on.

January 16: I phoned Maureen Birkland today. At first she refused to meet me for breakfast in the nearby café.

January 17: I have phoned seven times in the last hour. Miss Birkland is convinced now that I am Allen's father. She agrees to meet me tomorrow when her mother takes her brothers ice-skating.

January 18: I do not tolerate deception. The girl did not show up at the café, and so I went to her home. She was startled when she saw me. I did not have to tell her who I was.

She said, "You are Allen's father."

I can see why Allen was taken by her. She is a beautiful young woman with long tawny hair and wide intelligent eyes. She is frightened of me, but she is a proud young thing. But the home is that of a middle-class family—people without means. I do not intend to let her marry my son. I offered the girl ten-thousand dollars, and she threw the money back in my face. She told me I could not pay her enough to stay away from my son.

Allen groaned, but read on.

March 13: I flew south again today and went at once to the Birkland home. Packing crates and suitcases filled their living room. They are moving, but refuse to tell me where. But I saw the tag on one of the packing boxes: Running Springs.

I see Maureen's beauty in her mother, but the mother is sour. The girl was upstairs, leaning over the banister, staring down at me. She looked heavier, and I knew at once. The girl is pregnant. Pregnant with Allen's child.

I offered her mother ten-thousand dollars to take care of her daughter. She took the money and promised to give it to her daughter. Then she ordered me from her home. She told me that the Kladis family had already caused them enough grief.

April 7: I sit alone in my library in a darkened room with the curtains drawn. My wife cries at the door, begging me to comfort her. But there is no comfort. Today the navy notified us that Allen is dead. My son is dead. He is presumed drowned after an accident on a landing craft off Cyprus.

Allen, Allen, Allen. I had such plans for you, my son.

Some of Allen's rage slipped away. Even when he came home again, he never guessed how much his father had grieved for him. He tried to remember Alexander ever telling him that he loved him. He could not recall a time. Yet reading this journal, he realized that his father, in his own way, *had* loved him. But could that awareness erase what his father had done? Or erase the fact that Maureen had taken ten-thousand dollars from him? He thumbed through the journal. Only two or three more pages with his father's bold scrawl on them. The rest of the book was blank. He forced himself to finish reading what his father had written.

April 10: Sofia insists that we let the girl know that Allen drowned off the coast of Cyprus—that his body has not been found. Why would I tell the girl that? Why would I give Maureen Birkland the satisfaction that my son has died? But my wife is right. The girl has a right to know. After all, my son loved her.

April 12: I called the Birklands in Running Springs today. I heard Maureen's mother call to her daughter, and she was kind as she said, "Darling you must be brave. It's Allen's father."

May 1: When the mail came today, Sofia opened the last report from the investigator. She knows that there is an unborn child. Her grandchild. She insists that we send more money.

August 1: Almost a year since my son met that girl. The child should be born by now. I am relieved. The Birklands have moved away. I do not know where they are living now. But I have told Sofia that I sent money. That the girl is all right. But I have told her that the baby was stillborn. I can put it to rest now. With Allen gone, there will never be a paternity suit.

August 31: The State Department called today. Allen is alive! He has been held captive by the Turks. He has lost weight, but he is well. He is coming back. And inside I am confident that he will not find the girl in California even if he goes back to look for her. Allen is coming home. And all my dreams for my son are back on the drawing board.

September 1: Sofia has asked me to tell the girl that he is alive. I have promised to do so. Sofia will not ask me again.

Allen pressed his thumb and finger against his eyes, thinking, my father never kept that promise. When Allen opened his eyes again, his phone line was blinking. He pressed the intercom. "Vangie, I told you to hold all my calls."

"But your sister-in-law is here to see you and she won't leave until you do, Mr. Kladis. And she has five kids with her."

"Show them in." He stashed everything back into the folder and stowed it into his top drawer. He stood and went across the room to meet them. "Fran, this is an unexpected pleasure."

He grinned at the stair-steps lined up beside her, twins among them. The eldest one was almost sixteen, the youngest ten. A noisy handful, but he envied Nick and Fran. He shook hands with the eldest boy and tousled the heads of the others. "Hungry?" he asked.

"Yeah," the redheaded twelve-year-old announced. "Got some candy, Uncle Allen?"

"Not before lunch, Seth." He glanced at his wrist-watch. He poked his head out the door and, opening his wallet, said, "Vangie, can you get one of the secretaries to take the boys down to the cafeteria? Fran and I will join them later."

He looked back at the eldest boy. "Alex, you're in charge. Keep them in tow. If I get a good report, I might even ask Uncle Chris to take you down to the assembly line and let you sit in a plane."

"The super jets? All *right!*"

Alex herded his brothers into a line, tapping the youngest one with his knuckles the way Nick sometimes did. "Move it, Shortstop. See ya, Ma."

"I wish it were that easy at the house," Fran said. "There's no cooperation there."

"Then I'd better drop in more often."

"That's why I'm here. We're expecting you for dinner Sunday, and since you won't return your phone calls,

I'm here in person. Nick and I had it out last night, so he arranged for visitors' passes. If he'd only spend more time with the boys—''

"Sunday's on," Allen said.

"That includes church."

He nodded. "All right. I've been thinking about doing that anyway. Now, what is the real purpose of your visit?'' he asked as he gestured toward the chair across from his desk and settled back in his own.

She put her purse beside her chair, crossed her legs and faced him, her large eyes full of concern. "I'm worried about you, Allen."

"You've been worrying about me ever since Adrian died."

He admired Fran for having the courage to marry into the Kladis clan. Or maybe she had been too young to know better. She was an attractive spitfire of a lady, a foot shorter than Nick and rail-thin. But what did he expect? She'd been chasing kids since the first year of her marriage. She kept a good house, the cookie jar full, chauffeured the kids from one activity to another and tolerated her husband's demanding personality. She didn't need Allen to worry about on top of all that. But here she was—charming as they come and faithful as a watchdog taking him on.

"Allen, you've been avoiding us."

"I've been busy with the merger," he said. "And with Chris's encouragement, I started taking flying lessons in his Cessna. I'll be able to solo in another twenty hours."

"Are you trying to kill yourself before you meet Meggy?"

He folded his hands on the desk, his watch face visible. "Maureen didn't invite me to meet Meggy. I figure soaring above the clouds will help me forget this whole sordid mess.''

She threw her hands up in exasperation. "You're waiting for an invitation? You're a father, Allen. Be responsible. And you're in no state to be taking flying lessons. What's happening to you?"

"Chris flies."

"Chris was born to fly."

"And what was I born for, Fran?"

"You have to find that out for yourself. And the best way to do that is to get down to California and get this thing settled with Maureen and your daughter."

"I can't do that." His mouth twisted, his words breaking out. "Fran, do you know my dad paid Maureen off twenty years ago? Paid her so she wouldn't see me again?"

"That's over and done with. I'm talking about now."

"Did you and Nick know the truth all along?"

"We thought you knew. And we didn't want to cross your father. And after you met Adrian, it didn't seem to matter."

"How could it not matter—having a child of my own? Fran, you're a mother—you know what that means."

"Your father told us the baby was stillborn. Allen, I've always liked you. But not lately. Not since you let Maureen leave your condo without even trying to find out what really happened."

"She knew Dad owned Larhaven. She should have contacted me."

"Why would she do that? She thought you were dead."

Allen took the folder back out and slapped it on his desk. "But I have a child, and Maureen took ten-thousand dollars to keep the truth from me."

"It costs more than that to raise a child. I can't imagine what it was like to bear Meggy alone—thinking you were dead."

"My daughter knows I'm alive by now. She should call me."

Fran put her head back and laughed. "Allen Kladis, you are as arrogant as Nick. She doesn't know whether you want her or not. You have no such excuse."

"What am I to do?"

"I'd start by dialing the travel agency and ordering a ticket to Orange County on the first flight out."

"I'd miss Sunday dinner at your house."

"There'll be other Sundays. Don't let your daughter think you are rejecting her all over again."

"That was Maureen's doing."

"Perhaps. But for the last three days you've known about Meggy and you haven't done a thing about it except feel sorry for yourself."

He felt thimble-high as he braced against his leather chair. He closed his eyes, the receiver dangling from his hand and the dial tone buzzing. "I'd need Maureen's help, and I don't think she'd even talk to me—even if I flew down there."

"Fiddlesticks."

There was no arguing when Fran made up her mind. No arguing when he knew that she was right. He should make an honest effort to meet his daughter.

When he reached Orange County, he would confront Maureen. But this madness was not his fault. Even as he dialed the travel agency, Allen was still blaming Maureen, still nursing his own wounds.

Chapter Fifteen

In California Maureen spent her weekend alone, miserable because she had told Allen about Meggy in such an unforgiving way. For years, she had prided herself on being an expert in dividing her life into neat, compact departments—separating it successfully into her career, her social life, her speaking engagements, and her private moments that she guarded with great care.

Allen could not be compartmentalized. He stirred every fiber within her, aroused deep emotions. He was the one who would topple her career, the one who had stolen her heart. He belonged to her past, had crashed into her present, offered no promise to her future. And yet she loved him. She hated him. She adored him. She feared him. She needed him. Right now, the well-ordered compartments of her life were falling apart.

She had nowhere to turn. She dared not call Allen. Could not call Meggy. Refused to turn to Dwayne Crocker, no matter how gallant his offer of friendship. Instead, she turned blindly, foolishly to the telephone and dialed her mother in Cedar Lake.

The ringing sounded piercing. Her mother answered, stretching the word, "H-e-l-l-o, Ellen Birkland speaking."

Maureen forced herself to say, "Mother, it's Maureen."

"How nice of you to call."

As though she never called. Why didn't it work both ways? Why was Maureen left to keep in touch? She gripped the receiver. "Mother—"

"Is everything all right with you, dear?" There was just a hint of concern in her voice, yet more than a hint of impatience.

"Please help me, Mother."

Her mother's even breathing picked up. "You sound ill," she said in alarm.

Maureen brushed tears from her eyes, but she would not cry aloud. "I am," she whispered.

Her mother's momentary concern sharpened. "It's not Allen Kladis? Has he harmed you? Has he run out on you again?"

I'm the one running, Maureen thought. "I told Allen about Meggy."

"You fool!" The words exploded over the wire. "You know, his father paid you money never to tell him."

"Was that what the money was for? I thought it was to keep me away from Allen. Besides, his father gave you the money, Mother. You're the one who told Kladis that his son would never have to know the truth about the baby."

"And you think I was wrong?"

"I *know* you were wrong." She resisted telling her mother that the money, yellow with age, lay even now in her jewelry chest. "But I didn't call about Allen. I need your help to find my daughter."

Now her mother's fury awakened and poured over the wire, hurting her once again. "Don't start that again, Maureen."

"I need to know the name of the adoption agency, Mother. Is that too much to ask?"

"I threw it away."

The last three times the excuse had been different, her mother's opposition less vicious. "I don't believe you, Mother. You never throw away anything that's important."

"Find that daughter of yours and you make it difficult for your brothers and me. I won't hear of it. I won't be disgraced here in Cedar Lake or have this family scandalized again."

"All I want is the name of the adoption agency."

"You are asking too much. If you must find her, at least wait until I am dead."

She could imagine the proud tilt of her mother's chin, feel the opposition rising. But Maureen would not wait. At sixty-five and in good health, her mother could go on living for another ten or twenty years. "Mama, I want to find my daughter now—this year."

"Don't 'Mama' me. When you turned your back on me, young lady, and humiliated your family with that illegitimate child, you turned your back on God."

Her mother's words cut deeply, but Maureen lashed back. "I thought it was the same."

"God help you, child."

"I want Him to help me."

"Then you don't need my help."

"You won't even help me find your granddaughter?" Maureen asked softly. "She's part of you, too, Mama."

"Oh, Maureen, let it go. As far as I am concerned, I have no granddaughter. Just grandsons."

Had Maureen heard a catch in her mother's voice? But no. Ellen Birkland, proud woman that she was, had only paused for a breath. "You'd better find a nice quiet place and start praying, Maureen. You've waited long enough…"

Maureen choked on her mother's words, but knew in her heart that they were true. She no longer wanted to play church or mimic someone else's prayer. She wanted to find God, for if He did indeed see everything, then surely He could see Meggy even now. He alone knew where she was.

Without saying goodbye, Maureen replaced the receiver. Alone again, she knew that she would never be at peace until she found the child she had given away. But where would she begin?

Maureen collapsed on the divan, staining the teal-blue cushions with an unstoppable flood of tears. She was still there fifteen minutes later when her phone rang. She wiped her dry mouth, blew her nose, waited for the caller to give up. She could barely focus on the telephone. It kept ringing. Nine, ten, eleven rings. She tossed a pillow and missed.

Twelve. Thirteen. She had forgotten to turn the message machine back on. Fourteen. Fifteen. Slowly, she reached out and gripped the phone. "Yes," she said.

"Sis, it's Jason. I knew you had to be there."

Jason—twenty-seven, young, handsome, always driving in from Chicago to check in on their mother. Jason, who sent Christmas cards and birthday cards, and now and then called Maureen to see how she was. Jason keeping in touch in his own way.

"Did Mother call you, Jason?"

"No, I was here doing odd jobs for her. She keeps a list, you know. Keeps tabs on me that way. How are you, Maureen?"

"What do you think?"

"Sounds like you need a shoulder to cry on. And I've got a broad one. Admit it, Sis, you need your family."

"Oh, yes, I need the family all right. I never hear from Paul or Robert, and Mother and I always end up quarreling."

"It's a pattern that the two of you can't break."

"My fault, I suppose?"

"No one's blaming you."

"That's what Carl always told me."

"Wise man. I've thought about Carl a lot lately, Sis."

"So have I."

"I hated the way things turned out for the two of you. The truth is, I always hoped that you and Carl would have children."

"Carl didn't want children."

"Did he know about your daughter?"

"I told him before we married. He was philosophical about it. Told me he wasn't marrying my past, but me."

"He was a good man, Maureen."

"I know, but he got shortchanged when he got me. I didn't love him the way he deserved to be loved."

"The way I see it, you both gave it a good shot. You did your best. You just didn't have much in common."

She switched the receiver to her other hand. "He liked you, Jason. Said you were the best of the Birkland lot."

"Because I always went to his races."

"Racing was his whole life. I knew that when I married him. It was what he wanted to do. And he was good to me."

"I know."

"It just didn't work out. But you didn't call to talk about Carl, did you?"

Jason sent one of his easygoing chuckles over the wire. "Just thought we'd have one of those family chit-chats. Sis, what is it you need? What is it that upset Mother so? She's in her room with the door locked."

"I asked her for the name of the adoption agency—"

For a moment she thought the line had gone dead. Then he said, "I'll get it for you. I owe you that much. I still get ticked when I think about Mother coming back up to Running Springs and telling us the baby was gone. I thought she meant the baby was dead."

"Is that what Mother told you?"

He sighed. "Paul said you got rid of the baby. I was only seven or eight, Maureen. It was so much easier to think the baby was dead than to believe that you gave her away."

"She was adopted."

"It took me almost twenty years to find that out. Trying to get answers from Mom was like pulling teeth."

"Has she mentioned Allen lately?"

"Not in a kindly way. She about went bonkers when she found out he was still alive. Said he could only hurt you again. She's always been a proud woman, Maureen, but I never before realized she was so unfair."

The ominous note in his voice frightened Maureen. She sat huddled in the corner of the divan, pressing against the cushions...and waiting.

"Sis, a month ago a young woman called Mother, asking questions about you and Running Springs. Mother actually wrote down the girl's phone number and then threw the number away."

Maureen's throat ached. "My daughter?"

"We don't know. I drove down to Cedar Lake that

weekend. The minute I saw Mother, I knew something was up. That's when I heard the whole miserable story about giving the baby away.''

''I couldn't keep her. I had no way to take care of her....''

''I know that now,'' he said soothingly. ''I spent two hours going through the trash, hunting for that phone number. I still smelled like garbage when I called the girl back.''

There was a long pause. ''Mother had come back into the room by then, and she looked so wretched that I couldn't betray her. I ended up telling the girl that I didn't know anything about Running Springs. That my brothers and I grew up in Cedar Lake. I'm sorry, Sis.''

''Did you get her name, Jason?''

''No. I didn't ask. I just told her not to bother us again.''

''She may have been my daughter.''

''Mother argued that there was no way she could know about Cedar Lake. She said Allen was behind the call. I guess I believed her. And then we had a second phone call.''

''The same girl?''

''No, but yesterday a young man called me in Chicago. Said he was Brett Martin—asked me to meet him in Cedar Lake. If I didn't come, he was going to camp on Mother's doorstep.''

In the silence, Jason seemed to be weighing his words again. ''Mother was over in Anderson with Paul and his wife, so I refused to meet with Brett. But he knew your name, Maureen. Knew that you were part of this family.''

''What good will it do him if you turned him away?''

''He was nobody's fool. He threatened to go to the

Office of Vital Statistics. By now he knows when you were born, when you were married. What your married name is."

"And he's probably looking for me in Indiana. Was he a private investigator?"

"I think this was a personal matter with him. He said he was looking into things for his girl."

"Jason," she whispered, "did he call her by name?"

"If he did, I missed it. But somewhere out there, Maureen, I have a feeling your daughter is searching for you."

Small comfort, Maureen thought, a sob rising in her throat. How will she ever find me?

"I'm here for you, Sis. If I can help in any way—"

"Help me?" she anguished, her words brittle. "You may have just sent away my one chance of finding Meggy again."

Heather looked up as Brett barreled into the living room and slung his sweater over the chair back. He acknowledged Nan and Todd Reynard with a quick nod, and without embarrassment took Heather in his arms, held her tightly, and kissed her soundly.

She drew back, catching her breath. "When did you get back?"

"I just got in this afternoon and drove straight here."

"You're missing too many seminary classes."

"No, I canceled out of summer school."

"I didn't want you to do that." She patted the spot of the sofa beside her, and he sat down and slipped his arm around her.

"We have a time frame," he said evenly. "I don't want anything to stop our wedding in August. It may take us years to find your birth mother. We will go on looking, but I won't allow our search to stop our wedding next month. I love you, Heather. That's separate from finding your mother.''

Todd asked, ''Did you find your answers in Cedar Lake?''

Brett nodded. ''I have no doubt that the Birklands I talked to in Cedar Lake are related to Heather. They deny it, but they had too many questions—as though they wanted to be rid of me, but were reluctant to let me go. I'm certain the Jason I talked to was the younger brother in the family.''

''How can you be sure it was the right family?''

''So far, it's all we have to go on. Last weekend we were up to Running Springs again, Todd. We've been to the school the Birkland kids attended. There was no record of an older girl graduating. But there were three boys. Paul. Robert. Jason.''

Heather's gaze raced from Todd to Nan's troubled face. She ached for them. She had no words to convince them that they were still Mom and Dad—that she loved them fiercely.

''It took some doing,'' Brett said. ''But we did get some answers when we told them that the Birklands are family—that we want them at the wedding.''

Heather said, ''The wedding did it, Mom. The secretary at the school got all flustered and excited and said, 'Oh, an August wedding.' She went right to the files and came back with names. The Birklands were only in the school part of one year.''

Brett added, ''We tried the post office and the old neighbors again, and we found Jason's teacher. She was retired with nothing but memories to dwell on, but she was certain that the family moved to Indiana. The church organist pinpointed Cedar Lake. But this time we had the names of the kids. The teacher even remembered Jason talking about his big sister.''

"It didn't take much digging, Dad," Heather said. "Another woman near Running Springs home-schooled her. Said she was very young. Very pregnant." She paused, trying to fight back her tears. "She went down the mountain to have her baby and came back without it. Never said a word. They moved shortly after that.... I am certain I am the baby she was talking about."

Heather's voice softened to a whisper. "The church organist told us that my mother's name was Maureen."

"From the bits and pieces I learned in Indiana, I can add to that," Brett told them. "Heather's birth mother married some years later. The man's name was Carl Davenport."

He looked anxiously from Heather to her parents. "If the Davenports ever lived in Cedar Lake, there's no record of it. One thing I know for certain, she doesn't live there now. And if you can believe her brother Jason, there is no forwarding address."

Chapter Sixteen

Maureen took to the arrival of Fridays like a goldfish takes to water. It hadn't always been that way. She had been married to her job more years than she cared to remember, and was often guilty of stowing unfinished tasks in her case and taking them home with her for her weekend entertainment. What else did she have to do when she failed to arrange a tennis match or a day at the golf course with friends, and especially when opening night for the Philharmonic Orchestra had already sold out for this evening's performance? She was destined to be cooped up at the condo this weekend, with not even an excuse to scrub the kitchen. She had a day girl who dusted and scoured twice weekly, leaving the condo spotless. She could bake—something she enjoyed doing—but cookies grew stale in her cookie jar.

Before she could make her Friday escape, she still had a brief conference with Roland Spencer and Dwayne Crocker to contend with. They finally arrived—Dwayne with his cordial grin, and Roland looking striking in his colonel's uniform with its rows of ribbons.

"You're looking great, Davenport," the colonel greeted her.

"Roland, I just looked in the mirror. Besides, you saw me at the board meeting this morning."

"And just my luck, from the opposite end of the table." His square face looked ruddy now and his broad brow sported his usual scowl. "Crocker told me what's happening here at Fabian. Don't forget, when your job folds here, I can get you on in Washington."

She smiled up at him. "Just like that?"

"Just like that."

"The Pentagon! I may take you up on it. But not right away."

He was a cut above his contemporaries. Was it his uniform or just his pleasing personality?

She gave him a report on her visit to Seattle. "Mr. Kladis plans to increase the military contracts down here."

"Then he'll like the offers I just brought. But he's still letting you go, fool man."

"I may be one of the lucky ones. I won't wait for Allen to drop the ax—or to send a certified letter firing me."

"It sounds like a personal thing," the colonel said.

"As personal as you can get. I'm sure I'm on my way out."

"You're not a quitter, Maureen. This is just one of those tough, dry spells. I've seen you lick them before."

She stole a glance at his insignia. It always reminded her of an eagle ready to take flight, but she expected to see a star or two or three there before it was over. Roland would never quit. He was going for the top rank.

Colonel Spencer had known her ever since Carl—had even been at the race with her the day Carl died. He'd been like a rock then. He offered her his strong arm again now. "Why don't we cancel this conference and go out to dinner, make it a night on the town? You look like you could do with some cheering, girl."

Dwayne frowned. "Won't be much of a night out, Maureen. Roland's leaving on the red-eye for Washington."

"There's enough time to discuss those job possibilities in Washington over a good steak. You've got the right credentials."

"We'll use my car," Dwayne said. "You can leave your car here, Maureen. We'll swing back and pick it up later."

She didn't like the idea, but she agreed. "I have a couple of calls to make. I'll be down in a minute."

She stared at the door as it closed behind them. She was feeling neither hungry nor social. By the time they finished dinner, Roland would have her convinced that the cherry trees bloomed all year long in Washington and that golfing and tennis were part of the Pentagon routine.

Move to Washington? It would be a step higher. But would the glamour of life in the capital ever fill the emptiness she felt inside?

For years Maureen viewed her own climb up the corporate ladder as a redemptive, healing process—an effort to regain her mother's approval, to become more than she was, to prove her self-worth, to feel worthy of being loved again, and even to trust someone else to love her back. Dwayne? Roland?

No, she wanted *Allen* to love her back, but knew it was an elusive dream.

Always before, at each setback, she climbed harder. When she faced competition, she dug in more deeply, hung tough. When Carl died, she plunged into her work to ease her grief. In the back of her mind she thought that she could keep her sanity by being successful. Build her reputation by using her wit. Find peace at the top rung.

She saw the climb as futile now. Worthless. As little more than blind ambition. She wasn't climbing. She was running from the truth, running from the pain, stumbling over memories best forgotten. She was right back where it all began. Back to nothing. She had started from scratch, had clawed her way to the top—and it was over. It had begun with Allen; it had ended with him. It had begun at Fabian. She loved this job. Was challenged by the missile program and now it was slipping through her fingers.

As she locked her attaché case, she glanced out the window. Off in the far distance, a steel cross stood tall on a cathedral tower. She had an irresistible urge to kneel beneath it, to find out whether it really was level at the foot of the cross like her mother always said. The sight of that cross stirred a deep longing inside her. Was that the real key to redemption? Yes, she was certain of it. It wasn't what she did for herself, but the love and forgiveness that was freely given from God. She felt a measure of peace just standing there watching the sun-rings of sunset encircle the cross, felt the profound truth touch her life. But she didn't quite know how to absorb it, how to respond.

Her desk phone rang. Agitated at the disturbance, she grabbed the receiver. "Yes," she said.

"Mrs. Davenport? This is the security guard at the main gate. Mr. Crocker said for you to hurry. They're waiting."

"I'll be right down."

The spell was broken, but she had just latched on to a concept. The cross meant forgiveness. That was part of the healing process. Forgiveness. She knew what she must do.

She had to find Meggy.

It was late when they reached the condo. Still, Dwayne begged for a cup of coffee. "I won't stay," he promised.

Inside, he followed her into the kitchen, watched like one intrigued as she popped two cups of water in the microwave and set out two packets of cappuccino.

"I read a good article about the Indy 500 yesterday," Dwayne said. "It talked about some of the fatalities in the past. Carl Davenport was one of them."

"I know. What's the point, Dwayne?"

His gaze flicked nervously around the room. "It gave a bit of Carl's history. When he was born, married. And it said he had no children—"

She felt an icicle stab her heart.

"—but three months ago during dinner," he continued, "you told me you had a child. I assumed Carl Davenport was the father."

"I think you'd better go," she said calmly.

He twirled his empty cup. "I'm your friend, Maureen. I'd like to be more. One thing I don't like is someone hurting you. Something's going on—maybe between you and Allen Kladis."

"Nothing is going on."

"But something did in the past, didn't it? Maureen, I know it's none of my business. But something is troubling you, something besides holding on to your job at Fabian."

"And if I told you you're right, what then?"

"Then I could help you. We've been colleagues for a long time, and I've never seen a time when you weren't in control, or easily back into it. We fight you, but the men at Fabian respect you, Maureen. You always carry your full share. More than your share." He gave her another admiring glance. "You haven't even come close to the big four-o, and look how far you've come already."

"Why all the compliments at midnight?"

"It's not often I like a woman with brains. But you're more than that to me. I want to help out any way I can." His long fingers drummed on the table. "There's nothing that can't be solved with the right mathematical calculations."

He was getting close to the truth. Should she tell him about Meggy? While she pondered that one, the intercom buzzed.

"Thank goodness you're here. I don't like midnight callers."

"I'll check it out." He sauntered to the intercom. When he turned back, he was frowning. "Were you expecting Kladis?"

"Allen? Of course not. I wasn't expecting anyone."

"Well, that's who just buzzed in. He's on his way up. And he suggested that I put distance between us."

"No," she said, alarmed. "Stay. I may need a buffer zone."

"Do you want to tell me what happened?"

"What happened was twenty years ago."

He whipped off his glasses and wiped them with his tie. "Does it have to do with the child?"

"Yes, and it's something I must tell Allen."

When Dwayne opened the door, Allen said, "I told you to leave, Crocker."

"Can't. Haven't finished my coffee."

Allen stepped around Crocker, and when he did, Maureen could see the fire in his eyes, the taut lines around his mouth.

"Allen," she asked, "what do you want?"

"I just need Meggy's address."

"You flew all the way down from Seattle to ask me for an address? How could you afford to get away from Larhaven?"

"I'm the boss, remember? CEO and chairman and director and their biggest stockholder."

"In other words," she said sardonically, "you do what you want."

"Exactly."

"How long are you in town?"

He glared at Crocker, who was balancing another cup of coffee. "I'm staying as long as it takes to get acquainted with my daughter. If I have to, I can fly down on weekends—flying in on Friday evenings, heading back first thing Monday morning."

"You'd better sit down, Allen," she said.

"I won't bother you that long. Just tell me where Meggy is."

She rubbed her hands together, trying to keep them from trembling. Looking up into Allen's troubled face, she could not hate him. "I don't know Meggy's address. I haven't seen her since she was three days old."

She heard the hoarse rattle in his throat. "She's *dead?*"

"No. She was adopted twenty years ago."

Dwayne's cup crashed to the floor. He bent to pick it up, then mopped up the damp spot with a paper napkin. "I think I'd better go, Maureen. Will you be all right?"

"Yes. Thanks for coming, Dwayne."

He turned to Allen. "Don't bother looking for a hotel at this hour. I have an extra room."

Allen didn't seem to hear him. He sank onto the cushioned sofa and buried his face in his hands. "First Adrian. And now Meggy. I've lost them both."

From the doorway, Crocker said, "I'll wait in the car for you, Kladis. You'd do better at my place than alone at a hotel."

"It's all right," Maureen told him. "He'll be all right."

"I'll wait in the car just to be sure. But stay cool. You two are going to need each other if you plan to find your daughter."

"Get out," Allen said.

"I'm going. But the lady in the apartment next to mine works for Social Services. I think she could help you."

As the front door closed behind Crocker, Allen said, "You gave our baby away. My daughter. How could you, Maureen? *Why?*"

She paced back and forth in front of the sofa. "Mother made the decision, Allen. I was still seventeen, with no rights of my own."

"That's no excuse. Everyone seems to know about my daughter except me."

"Nick knew. Why didn't he tell you?"

"He claims he thought I knew. Besides, he was told our child had died."

"Well, I believe she's very much alive, and according to my brother Jason, she may be searching for us. I have the name of the county adoption agency. It's not much, but it's all we have to go on. And if we are going to work together—"

"I'm not here to discuss the merger between our companies."

"Nor am I. But we have to put away our differences if we are to find Meggy…. God surely knows where she is."

"Where was God when you gave our daughter away?"

"Where were you?" she countered in a whisper. "Allen. I think you'd better take Dwayne up on his offer. You need a good night's sleep. Tomorrow is Saturday—we can sit down like rational human beings and talk it over."

Allen didn't look any better in the morning, but at least his head was clear. He spread his hands over the memo pad on Maureen's kitchen table and plotted a course of action. He had taken charge. She resented it and yet felt relief at the same time.

"The way I see it," he said, "we have several places to start. The hospital where she was born, the Vital Records Office—every county should have one—the court house, a lawyer's office. Reeny, if you could just remember the name of the people who adopted her, we'd have something to go on."

She felt a stab of guilt. She had taken their flesh and blood, and turned her over to total strangers. And in exchange, Maureen had nothing. No name. No link to the people who adopted her baby.

"You can ask my mother, but I doubt that you will find any cooperation there."

"Well, Dwayne's keeping a level head. He'll do what he can to get us an appointment with a social worker. If we can just get some cooperation there—" Then, eyeing her, he said, "Are you okay, Reeny? You look a bit pale."

"I didn't sleep well last night."

She hadn't slept at all. She had showered and paced, and when she had exhausted herself with tears, she showered again, standing under the hot steam, willing the void inside her to fill.

His tone mellowed for a moment. "You were thinking about Meggy, weren't you?"

"Yes." And about you, she thought. Longing for Meggy. Doubting that we would find her. Thinking about all of the might-have-beens. Hating you, Allen. Loving you.

Allen jabbed the memo pad. "There had to be an order of adoption. Some kind of a consent decree. You must have signed something, Maureen. What other names were on those papers?"

"I don't know. And, Allen, I will not let you run me into the ground. I can search for Meggy without you. My days at Fabian are numbered, and once I leave there, I can devote myself full time. And I will…. Now, we can work together or we can go our separate ways. It's your choice, but please don't treat me like one of your employees."

With a great measure of calm, he said, "We'll work together."

He reached out and covered her hand with his, a gentle gesture characteristic of the old Allen—the man who still made her heart do cartwheels inside her.

She pulled free. "We'll need to work on this on weekdays, too, Allen. These agencies will be closed on weekends."

"If I have to, I'll take some vacation time from work. I'll hire a private investigator if need be."

"What about the merger?"

"Finding Meggy is priority, Reeny. We have a daughter out there somewhere who needs to know we care about her."

Although Allen had sounded calm during the original discussion, his mood exploded the following Friday when they met with the hospital administrator where Meggy was born.

"The records are sealed," the man said. "Twenty years ago, you say?"

"We gave you her birth date," Allen snapped.

"Yes, I see. She was twenty years old a few days ago. But her records are hospital business and they are sealed. You should try the records at the newspaper archives."

"We did. It listed her as 'Baby Girl Birkland,' and it listed this hospital as the place of her birth," Allen argued.

"And in the case of Mrs. Davenport here, her hospitalization would be on microfiche, if we have kept it at all." He stood, dismissing them. "If you're through, I have other appointments."

Back out in the hospital parking lot, Maureen said, "Allen we're not going to get anywhere with you yelling at everyone we talk to."

"Well, what right do they have to tell us we can't see the records on our own daughter? It's the same thing the woman at the Bureau of Records told us. And that judge refusing to help us—"

"We'll try him again," she said. "I keep wondering, Allen, is there any way you can get help through the military? Our child was born when you were missing in Cyprus. You just now found out about her. Maybe—"

"That's a shot in the dark."

"What else do we have to go on?"

"Reeny, what happens if we never find her?"

She knew he was right. Sometimes the lost child was never found.

In the middle of August, with their personal problems still unresolved and the merger of their companies still not finalized, Dwayne Crocker came up with the solution. He strolled into the condo and said, "You know that social worker I told you about?"

Allen nodded. "Your neighbor. What about her?"

"She said you need to go into the agency that handled her adoption and sign a release form giving your name and address. That way if your daughter or the people who adopted her begin a search of their own, they know you're willing to be found."

"We're not lost," Allen said. "Meggy is."

"Consider it from their viewpoint. My neighbor thinks she's tracked down the agent who handled your daughter's adoption."

"How would she know that?"

"By snooping around. She owed me one. I keep her appraised of good stock investments—some have paid off." He smiled. "So do you want the lady's name and address or not?" He dangled a piece of paper in the air, his bony fingers wrapped around it. "According to my neighbor, you don't have much time to follow through. They're throwing a retirement party for this woman in a few days. She didn't want to take appointments, but we got you one anyway."

Allen snatched the paper. "We're on it," he said.

Chapter Seventeen

$\smallsmile$

Maureen studied the clear cut of Allen's Grecian profile: a finely shaped nose, a strong brow, the firm chin. His heavy lids drooped with weariness; the rich dark eyes seemed more like burning coals. These last few weeks had aged him. He looked tired, pensive, and she ached for him. Her own keen disappointment at not finding Meggy had become agonizing, unbearable. What must it be for Allen? He was a man accustomed to making decisions, to reaching his goals—a man who didn't accept failure.

He glanced up from the divan and saw her watching him. A crooked smile tugged at the corner of his mouth. "I'm sorry, but my board of directors at Larhaven are putting the pressure on. They want me to cut back on my visits down here until after the merger."

"I understand. If anything happens, I'll let you know."

"I don't like running out on you, Reeny."

She smiled inwardly. Isn't that what you always do? she thought.

"I thought that appointment at the social worker's was our answer to finding Meggy. I counted on it. But it's the third week in August...and nothing. We haven't heard a word from Miss Wagner since that interview."

"That was her last day at work, Allen."

"But she promised to write out a report of our visit and to make certain the permission slips to contact us went into our daughter's file. What if she mislaid them?"

"She was too efficient for that."

"She probably didn't find her purse that day. The room was a clutter, nothing but half-filled boxes and packing crates."

"She meant well."

"Did she? She scared me to death, Reeny. She was stern and clinical. She never did admit whether she handled Meggy's case."

"I recognized her. She was older, but she was the same woman who carried my baby out of the hospital."

"You're sure? There was no recognition on her part."

"I clearly remember her handing me the consent papers, urging me to sign them. I remember her stern expression, staring down at me. She didn't smile—"

"She didn't smile the other day either."

The Reynard's home was a buzz of activity when Brett Martin walked in through the back door. "I got here as soon as I could," he said. "Is Heather all right?"

"She's in the living room with her father—and a guest. Tell Todd I will be right in with cookies and coffee."

He gave Nan a peck on the cheek, dropped his jacket on the kitchen chair, and bounded toward the living room. Heather was on her feet, going straight into his arms and turning his worries into a smile.

"You're okay, Heather?"

"Never better. But I want you to meet someone."

She nodded to the guest, sitting stiffly in the over-stuffed chair—a beautiful, well-dressed woman with smooth, ebony skin. She was studying Brett with unsmiling eyes.

"Miss Wagner, this is my fiancé, Brett Martin."

A faint smile touched her mouth. "The preacher?" she said, taking his hand and shaking it warmly.

"I will be in another year or two. But you have an advantage on me. I don't know who you are."

Heather jumped in. "She's a social worker."

"Retired," the woman said. "Otherwise, I could not be here. It would be unethical." Her eyes were back on Heather. "Your parents tell me you're to be married soon. You're so young."

"But I'm so sure, Miss Wagner. I really do love Brett."

"Your parents will miss you," she said, as Nan joined them with the promised tray of coffee and cookies.

"They'll miss my clutter. But we won't be far away. Just two or three hours in heavy traffic."

Nan shook her head. "But we have no idea where the two of them will settle down once Brett takes his first pastorate."

Heather laughed. "That's a long time from now. But Miss Wagner didn't come to talk about our wedding, Brett. She's here to tell us about my birth mother."

"You've found her?"

"We're not certain," Miss Wagner said, "but we think so."

"Oh, sit down, Brett. Don't pace. Let Mom and Dad and Miss Wagner tell us everything."

Miss Wagner nodded toward the Reynards. "Your parents came to see me several times in the last few weeks, begging me to help them find your birth mother. I told them that the records were closed. That I could do nothing."

"Then why are you here?" Brett asked.

"The day I retired, another couple came to see me. I am confident they were looking for you, Miss Reynard. But when I wrote a report of their visit, I was told that it would make no difference. Your records would remain sealed. It wasn't fair."

"That's when Miss Wagner called us," Todd interjected.

"Twenty years of working with the agency. Twenty years of watching young mothers give up their children. It made the men and women who adopted them joyful, but just once I wanted to see all of them get together again." She massaged an arthritic hand. "I should not be here. I would not be if I were still working for the adoption agency."

Brett smiled. "Sounds like you want a clear conscience."

"I recognized Mrs. Davenport when she came to my office. She was one of the first young mothers I worked with. She was Maureen Birkland then. But I don't think she recognized me."

"You said a 'couple' came to you," Heather said.

"Yes. You see, your father is not dead," she said gently. "I talked to him. His name is Allen Kladis."

She smiled now for the first time as she turned to Nan and Todd Reynard. "When I arrived this afternoon, I recognized your home. I must have come here for several visits before the adoption. And many after you took Heather home.''

"Why did you come so many times?'' Brett asked.

"After they filed the papers to adopt, I was assigned as their caseworker. It was my job to walk them through the adoption.''

"I figured she was here to see what we were made of,'' Todd said. "To see if we'd qualify. To try and talk us into an older child. To make certain you'd have a room of your own, Heather.'' He shook his head. "Every time she came, I kept wondering what she put into that great big notebook of hers.''

"My heart,'' Miss Wagner said. "It was always difficult to place a child. I feared making mistakes that I would have to live with.''

Tears welled in Nan's eyes. "I'll never forget the day that Miss Wagner called us and told us we had a baby girl. But you were already in our hearts before that phone call. You were six-and-a-half pounds of pure joy.''

"What I remember about Mr. Reynard—about your father—was putting you into his arms that first time. I can still remember him saying, 'This is the most beautiful baby I ever saw.'''

Miss Wagner searched Heather's face. "You have grown into a very lovely young woman. When I called your parents the other day, I told them that I was certain I had found your birth parents. I asked what they wanted me to do. They told me you were to know the truth— that you were the one to make the decision.''

She leaned forward and handed Heather an index card with a name and phone number on it. "If you decide to contact your birth mother, it's best to have someone else initiate the call. That way, if there are other children, or there is reluctance—''

Heather was already on her feet, pulling Brett up beside her. "Come with me," she said. "I'm going to call Maureen Davenport right now and invite her to our wedding."

It was just past seven when Maureen's phone rang.

"Don't answer it," Allen said, his arm pressed against his forehead as he leaned back against her sofa.

"It might be important."

"It might be Dwayne Crocker. I don't need him popping in this evening."

The ringing stopped. "I should have answered, Allen."

"If it's important, they'll call back."

Five minutes later, the piercing ring echoed through the room again. Allen bolted upright and leaned forward. Maureen met his gaze.

"Reeny, let the machine pick it up. Then we'll know who it is."

"But I turned the answering machine off."

She took up the handset on the seventh ring. "Hello," she murmured, her voice wary.

She could hear someone breathing on the other end of the wire as though the caller were weeping, uncertain. There were voices in the background, urging her to "go gently." And then a sweet voice said, "Hello."

"Who is this?" Maureen asked. "How may I help you?"

She almost responded to the silence by hanging up. Then the young woman on the other end of the line asked softly, "Mrs. Davenport?"

"Yes."

"Mrs. Maureen Davenport?"

"Yes." Maureen's second *yes* was more abrupt. She felt a tightening in her gut. Her thumping heart skipped a bit. "Yes, this is Maureen Davenport."

"I've been trying to find you for a long time. This is Heather Reynard.... I'm your daughter, Mrs. Davenport."

Chapter Eighteen

~❧~

Saturday. Maureen huddled against the passenger door,
her fingers nervously twisting Carl Davenport's diamond, as they sped down the Pacific Coast Highway
without speaking. She wasn't sure why she had worn
her rings, except that they were reminders to Allen that
someone had wanted her, and would be symbols for
Meggy that Maureen had not always been single.

Earlier that morning Maureen had gone to her office
at Fabian, surprising the guard at the gate.

"Working today, Mrs. Davenport?"

"Not today. I'm just picking up a few things."

She had opened her jewelry chest with great care, taking out the photo of newborn Meggy and staining it with
fresh tears.

Will I know you? she cried. Will I recognize you?
Surely the heart of a mother would know her child.

She tucked the picture into her purse, along with the
beaded baby bracelet that formed the words *Baby Birkland.*

As she lowered the lid, she spotted her diamond and

wedding band and, somehow needing a reminder of Carl's jovial lighthearted way, she slid the rings on her finger—on her right hand this time because Carl was gone.

The guard seemed even more surprised at how quickly she left the grounds. "Have a good day, Mrs. Davenport," he said as he waved her through the gated property.

A good day. Would it be a good day? How could it be anything but when she had lived for this moment for twenty years? She had taken hours to dress—outfits strewn across her bed as she tried on one summer suit after the other. Finally she had chosen a soft yellow pantsuit, as breezy and colorful as the day itself. But doing her face was even harder. She applied her makeup and smeared it with tears. She tried again, but the concealer did nothing for the dark circles beneath her eyes or the puffiness of her eyelids. She put on her favorite earrings and lipstick, and was ready when Allen arrived.

"Allen," she choked out, "we should take pictures of Heather—in case this is the only time we ever see her."

"Don't worry," he said stiffly. "I brought my camera."

But he had been preoccupied as he walked her back down the steps of the condo to the car, and now while driving. She ached for Allen sitting beside her, wearing a suit and tie on this miserably hot day. He looked more as if he was ready for a business meeting than a reunion with his daughter. His broad fingers wrapped tightly around the steering wheel. He made a handsome figure, dark and intense, keeping his thoughts and feelings wrapped inside him. But then, he had had only a few weeks to wonder about his daughter. Only a few weeks to cram a lifetime of longing for her into this hour.

"There it is, Allen. Around the next curve."

He accelerated, and as they rounded the granite cliff, they saw the hotel-restaurant perched high above the Pacific Ocean. She knew that they were only a few miles from the sandy beach where they had first met, but it could have been across the Great Divide, so separated had they become in these last few days.

Allen pulled into valet parking and grabbed his camera from the glove compartment. "We're looking for Windy Bluff," he told the attendant.

The young man pointed toward a rocky precipice. "It's out that way. A good quarter of a mile. It's a spectacular view, but the path is narrow, the drop-off steep, and the wind at the bluff will just about blow you over."

Maureen shuddered. "I didn't even bring a sweater or walking shoes."

"We'll go slowly. And you can have my coat if you need it."

The trail was steep. She considered kicking off her heels, but didn't want to meet her daughter in her stocking feet. As they neared the bluff, the view was breathtaking. Far down the cliff, the waves crashed over the rocky coast.

Just beyond the ridge, Maureen saw the lone couple standing there on the bluff, windblown as they faced the ocean. It had to be Heather, with a rangy young man at her side.

She grabbed Allen's arm for support, and he did not resist. "They're just standing there," she whispered.

"So we go to them."

As they drew nearer, the couple turned. Maureen gasped. "Allen, she has your eyes."

He smiled back. "And she has your beauty."

Maureen stopped because she could go no farther. Her heart pounded as wildly as the ocean waves thundering against the rocks. This was her *daughter*. She would have known Meggy anywhere. Allen snapped a picture as she stood there, her hair ruffled by the wind. And now their daughter was laughing, crying and radiant as she came to them with her arms wide-open.

"I'm Heather," she said as she released them.

"You are so lovely," Maureen said.

Heather laughed. "I was just going to say the same thing to you. I think I look like you."

"But you have Allen's eyes."

Heather looked up into her birth father's eyes and flicked back her hair—hair as black as Allen's. "I think we have a match," she told him.

He nodded, his eyes moist.

Heather turned and beckoned for the young man to join them. "This is Brett," she said with pride. "He helped me find you."

Brett extended his hand. He had a strong grasp. A strong face. A comforting smile. His hair was as wind-blown as Heather's, but he was towheaded and fair-skinned.

"I'd invite you to sit down," he said, "but all we have to offer are rocks for chairs."

Heather looked anxious. "I'm sorry. I guess we should have met at the hotel or in the restaurant, like Brett wanted to do, but I wanted the place to be special. I just wanted to be away from the crowds when I met you."

"It's beautiful here, Heather," Maureen said. Almost as lovely as you are, dear Meggy, she added silently.

Allen spread out his coat for a throw rug, and allowed

Maureen and his daughter to sit down on it. Awkwardly, wordlessly, they tried to find comfort on the hard ground. Finally, Heather asked, "You're not disappointed, are you?"

Maureen shook her head. "No, just overwhelmed. I've dreamed of this moment for twenty years, Meggy— I mean *Heather*."

A look of delight filled Heather's face. "Did you know my middle name was Megan? Is that why you called me Meggy?"

"Megan was the name I was going to give you. But I always thought of you as Meggy."

"Then you did think of me?"

"All the time."

"Todd—that's my dad—wanted to name me Heather," she mused. "But Nan—that's my mom—insisted that my middle name be Megan. She said someone special asked her to call me that." Her gaze was direct. "Did Mom and Dad know that you wanted to call me Megan when I was born?"

Maureen could hardly breathe. "The social worker knew."

"Brett says you had to love me because you went through that long pregnancy for me. And now you tell me you wanted to name me. If you cared that much, then why did you give me away?"

Maureen felt as though a saber had been thrust through her heart. Allen groaned beside her. She touched his knee for support. "I thought Allen was dead—and I was only seventeen."

Allen's voice was controlled. "And her mother insisted that she give you away. That she not try to raise you alone."

"It was the hardest thing I ever did, Meggy." Maureen hesitated. "I'm sorry. I called you Meggy instead of Heather."

"That's okay. I think I'd like you to call me that, now that I know why." Heather patted Maureen's tear-stained cheek. "It's all right. Now that I know the whole story, somehow it makes everything easier."

"Have you been happy?" Allen asked.

"Oh, yes. I have wonderful parents. Godly people. Kind people. They wanted me—"

Maureen gasped. "I'm so sorry."

"I didn't mean it that way. I just meant—"

Brett said, "She just meant that they really wanted her. They're good people. It should help both of you to know that. Heather has no real regrets. Neither do I."

"We do," Allen said. And then, apologetically, he told them about going back to find Maureen.

"Then you were going to marry each other?"

"Yes, but Maureen wasn't there when I went back to find her. We came here today to learn everything we could about you."

"That's a long story," Brett quipped.

And so they told them about Heather's childhood—about a happy little girl who went to church and Sunday School, and excelled all through grade school. Heather told them about her friends, and about Girl Scouts and how she ate most of the cookies instead of selling them. She talked about loving pizza and chocolate ice cream, and about having chicken pox, and about her dad's first heart attack and how scared she was when she almost lost him. She grew more serious when she told them about her rebellion in her junior year in high school, and the aching void inside when she wondered about her birth parents.

"The worst part was not knowing who I was or why

my mother went away. And being teased sometimes because I was adopted. But Todd and Nan were so special. They told me even Moses was adopted. They never stopped loving me. They saw me through measles and fusing and fuming and the slamming of doors and the winning of awards at school, and through swimming and skiing lessons. They even like Brett,'' she said proudly.

Abruptly, she said, ''Now it's your turn. Tell me about you.''

They told her about Running Springs and Cedar Lake, about Adrian and Carl, about the merger that had thrust them together again. They did not tell her that they were at odds, but Maureen was certain that Heather had figured out they were unhappy in each other's presence now. But Heather went on loving them, smiling at them, begging them to tell her more. To tell her everything.

''I want to know about you,'' she said, looking at Allen. ''Mom and Dad thought you had died in the navy.''

''There was a military incident in Cyprus,'' he admitted. ''And I was in captivity for several months. That's when Maureen moved back to Cedar Lake. That's how we lost contact.''

''Did you know about me?'' Heather asked softly.

''Not until a few weeks ago.''

Heather's gaze turned back to Maureen. ''Why didn't you tell him about me?''

''I moved away. We lost touch.''

''And she thought I was dead,'' Allen said soberly.

Maureen spared Allen the humiliation of telling Heather that his father had paid her to stay away from his son. Barely whispering, she said, ''If it hadn't been for the merger of your father's company and Fabian, I would never have known that Allen was still alive.''

Brett let sand course through his fingers. Without looking at anyone in particular, he said, "How sad for all of you."

"Yes," Allen agreed in a somber tone. They were all silent for a moment, then Allen said to Brett, "You know, I think we've met once before. In the airport, several weeks ago."

"That's right." Brett nodded. "No wonder you look familiar, sir. I was there to meet Heather when she flew in from Cedar Lake, and you were heading to the northwest. I asked you for the time."

"And told me all about your fiancée," Allen reminded him. "A strange coincidence. Just like my reunion with Maureen," he added.

Brett grinned. "You may see these events as purely chance. But I believe it's more. It's part of God's plan for your life."

Maureen briefly met Allen's gaze, then looked away. She did believe there was some deeper purpose to their reunion. But what it was exactly, she couldn't say. Was it just a chance to put the past to rest? To make Allen aware of Heather's existence and to find her? Or would there be a second chance for their love? More and more, Maureen felt that hope dwindle.

But she was relieved for Heather. It was the happy relief a mother feels, she realized, seeing that her daughter has made a good choice for marriage.

Brett was a quiet young man, saying little, absorbing everything, as sturdy as the rocky cliffs that surrounded them. It was obvious to Maureen that he was Heather's strength. Love flowed between them. The way it did between Allen and me when we were young, she thought.

"It was difficult trying to find a way to tell Allen

about Heather. And yet I was so excited when I saw him
again—''

"You mean you were still fond of him?'' Brett asked
perceptively.

She turned away from Allen so he could not see the
blush that crept over her face. "I was too ashamed to
tell him. How do you tell someone that you gave his
child away?''

Maureen snatched a handkerchief from her purse,
leaving the pink baby bracelet and the newborn photo
exposed. Across her open purse, she met Heather's gaze.

"Mine?'' Heather asked. "Oh, let me see them.''

She seemed to savor the feel of the tiny pink beads.
"Baby Birkland,'' she read aloud, and then looking at
the photo exclaimed, "I was such a funny-looking
thing.''

"No, you were beautiful to me.''

Brett peered over Heather's shoulder. "Yeah, kind of
cute.''

As Heather dropped them back into Maureen's purse,
she whispered, "You kept them all this time?''

"It was all that I had of you, Heather, except my
memories.''

Allen pressed his head against the rock cliff, his eyes
tearing, as Heather slipped her fingers around Maureen's. "I'm glad we found you. I've waited all my life,
Maureen, to know what it was like the day I was born.
What it meant to you to carry me in your womb. Can
you tell me?''

Should she confess that she wept through much of her
pregnancy? Wept for fear her mother would find out,
cried later because Allen was gone. "I can't... Not now.
Please. I only knew you for the first three days of your

life." She tossed her sodden handkerchief onto the sand and grabbed a dry one.

Brett kissed the top of Heather's head. "Honey, I think it may be too soon for her to tell you that. Besides, it's getting late. I think we'd better go now."

The sea crashed against the rocks as the men pulled the women to their feet. Brett caught Heather in his arms; Allen shook the sand from his jacket and put it around Maureen's shoulders. "That's on loan until we get back to your condo."

"Heather, will we see you again?" Maureen asked.

"There won't be much time," Heather apologized. "Do you realize we've been together three hours, and I'm still not sure what I should call you. You're my birth parents, but it's—"

"Why don't you call me Maureen?"

"And Allen," Allen said, his voice husky.

Heather glanced up at Brett, love in her gaze. "There's something we haven't told you. You see, Brett and I are getting married next Saturday."

Brett winked. "And after that, you won't see us for three weeks. And we won't be taking any phone calls."

Heather's cheeks were on fire. Blushing, she said, "After our honeymoon, Brett goes back to seminary for his last year."

Allen looked morose. "By then, I'll be back in Seattle," he said.

Again she looked up at Brett. "I could catch a bus to the northwest. We could fit that into our budget, couldn't we? You'll be in school, but I could go up and see Allen for a few days."

Allen reached out and touched his daughter's cheek. "That's sweet. But you'll be on your honeymoon for a long time."

"Maybe I can switch runs with one of the flight attendants."

"We'll work something out. We're not going to let this be the grand finale," he promised.

"Do you have a family up there, Allen?"

"Just brothers. But I'm alone since Adrian's death— we had no children." He smiled uneasily. "You're my only daughter."

"But you're staying in the area, aren't you, Maureen?"

"I'll be leaving my job at Fabian soon." Her glance at Allen was peppery, yet long enough to see that his jaw was set, his eyes averting hers. "I may move back to Cedar Lake, Indiana."

Allen responded then. "That should make for a miserable existence. I hope you're not moving in with your mother?"

"Would it matter?"

"Things may not have worked out for us, Maureen, but I want you to be happy."

Do you? she wondered. How can I ever be happy without you?

"Maureen," Heather interrupted, "Brett and I want you and Allen to come to our wedding."

"Of course, I'll be there, Heather."

Allen agreed. "I'll stay on for the occasion."

As Allen snapped a closeup of Heather, she brushed her unruly hair from her face. "We can't ask you to do anything special. Everything's arranged. Todd is giving me away, and Nan pretty much has everything else organized."

From the depth of her own pain, Maureen managed a smile. She would be at her daughter's wedding as the unknown guest, sitting beside the birth father of the bride and barely speaking to him. She struggled to link the infant child that she had held with this beautiful young woman who had Allen's eyes and dark hair.

But she would be there for the wedding! It was more than she had ever dreamed! "We understand, really we do, dear. Thank you for inviting us. But will we see you before Saturday?"

The breeze whipped Heather's hair across her face again. Behind her, the setting sun turned the ocean into golden hues. The glow radiated on Heather's face, giving a luster to her cheeks and making her seem even more vulnerable. The sound of the sea waves filled the silence.

In spite of the churning water crashing on shore, Maureen had a measure of peace in that moment that time could never take away. She had seen her daughter and recognized her in an instant—and in that moment of recognition, she loved her as she had loved her all these years. She would hold this memory in her heart, no matter what happened.

"Maureen," Heather said softly, "Mom and Dad want you to come to dinner on Tuesday. So we can talk things over. How things will work out. Where you will sit. Whether you will be introduced at the reception. The first two rows will be family. Nan and Todd well, we have a lot of aunts and uncles."

"Why not sit on the groom's side," Brett offered.

"No, Brett, they belong on the bride's side. That's settled. I'll ask Mom to save the third row for them."

Allen frowned. "Look, if there's a problem with the seating…"

Maureen touched Allen's hand to silence him. She knew he was used to being in charge. He was dealing with this in his own way, guarding his emotions, afraid to feel too deeply. "Go on, Brett. What were you saying?"

"I was trying to explain how important it is to Heather to have you there. But you have to meet the Reynards so things will go smoothly. It will be a big wedding—a lot of people."

"We promise to be on our best behavior," Allen said wryly.

"Just having you there is what matters." Heather's eyes were on Maureen again. "I didn't know that my birth father was still alive until the other day. But all my life I've wondered about you, Maureen. Wondered where you were. Why you went away."

Tears stung behind Maureen's eyes.

"You don't have to tell me now. But maybe someday." Her voice grew tender. "I love Mom and Dad. No parents could have been more loving. But I've had something missing inside. That's why I insisted on finding you."

"So you could invite us to your wedding?"

"We had some practical reasons, too," Brett said. "We plan a family. But Heather didn't want any children until we knew the medical background of her birth parents."

A genetic accounting, Maureen thought. Is that all these dear young people wanted? She felt Allen bristle beside her.

"We have no mental illnesses or chronic diseases, if that's what worries you."

"We're not worried, sir. We'll take whatever medical history you have. But Heather had another reason for searching for you."

"You tell them, Brett. You're the future preacher."

"No, they need to hear it from you."

Again Maureen was cognizant of this moment in time as though she were snapping another mental picture of Heather and her fiancé to carry her through the lonely years ahead. Measured in inches, they were barely more than two feet apart. But how would she ever bridge the gap? Would Allen? What was wrong with him? Couldn't he see Heather's heart—how she longed for his acceptance?

"I'm waiting," Maureen said gently.

"Three months ago I told Brett that I had to find you before our wedding. I wanted you there. But even more I wanted you to know that I forgave you for giving me away—and that even without knowing you, I loved you."

Maureen's hands went to her mouth, stifling a sob.

"I was certain of Brett's love, and Nan and Todd's love, but I didn't know where I stood with you, or where you were." She glanced at Allen. "I never thought about loving you—I thought you were dead. But I think I can love you if you will let me."

Allen nodded, restrained tears tracking down his cheeks.

Brett's arm tightened around Heather, and she shot him a grateful smile. "Go on," Brett said. "Tell them the rest."

"Maureen—Allen, I wanted to meet you at least once just so I could tell you that God loves you very much. That Christ died for you. That He...wants you to believe in Him."

"A sermon in a nutshell." Allen faced them again. "I've been getting that from all sides lately. Even from my sister-in-law."

"Good!" Brett said. "Now, what about dinner at the

Reynard's on Tuesday? Your mom said around seven, didn't she, hon?"

"That's right, and she likes to eat on time and then sit around the table and talk." She laughed. "She'll want to tell you a little bit about the joys and trials she's had in raising me. You will come, won't you?"

"We'll be there," Allen said.

Maureen embraced her daughter. "This has been the most wonderful day of my life."

"I'm glad it happened. I'm glad we've found each other."

Maureen watched them go, arm in arm up the winding path toward the hotel parking lot. They didn't look back, and Maureen was grateful. She didn't want them to see her crying again, didn't want them to see Allen strolling on ahead of her.

Chapter Nineteen

Maureen slipped into a sleek, off-the-shoulder silk dress, very elegant and slimming, the azure highlighting the velvet blue of her eyes. She wiggled her polished toes into three-inch heels and then stepped back to survey herself in the mirror. Dressy, but not *too* dressy. Casual, but not *too* casual. Tall enough to come an inch above Allen's shoulder, an eye-to-eye encounter when she wouldn't have to think he was looking down at her. She removed the locket and thin gold chain from around her neck, and replaced it with the long strand of pearls that Carl Davenport had given her on their first wedding anniversary. Then she studied herself in the mirror again.

She realized now that for the last few days she had been subconsciously wearing things and doing things that would remind Allen of Carl, in the same way that Allen's presence constantly reminded her of Adrian. She applied fresh shell-pink lipstick and was ready when the doorbell rang.

She turned out the lights on the way and swung the

door open, praying that they could maintain a facade of friendship this evening for Heather's sake.

Allen stepped into the room, approval in his eyes. "You look great, Reeny."

She surveyed the sharp cut of his tweed blazer and well-creased dark slacks. His broadcloth dress shirt and striped silk tie were equally expensive. She focused on his well-chiseled face, strong and handsome, freshly shaven and scented with that tangy cologne that seemed so much a part of him. "You don't look too shabby yourself."

"You don't think we're overdressed, Maureen?"

"We'll know soon enough. For Heather's sake I hope we don't embarrass her." She picked up her purse. "I'm ready."

"No offer of a cup of tea to build up my courage? I feel like a man about to meet his in-laws."

"In a way, we are. Let's forget the tea and go straight on. We may have to look for the place, and we don't want to be late."

"I have a faint suspicion that all we have to do is pick the most luxurious home on the highest bluff, and we're there."

"Allen, Heather said they had an ocean view. That's all. She was too down-to-earth to have been schooled in private academies or to have lived in a gated community. Now let's go."

"I feel a bit nervous about meeting the people who raised Heather," he confessed.

She twisted the pearls as he locked the door for her. "We should be grateful to them. I think they've done a beautiful job. I just hope they like us, Allen."

He twirled the key chain on his finger and handed it back to her. "The truth is, I don't even feel comfortable with Heather yet. It's a tough one. She's twenty. Grown up. Getting married. And I haven't even had time to get used to the idea that she exists."

"Well, she does," Maureen said softly as he led her down the steps to the curb. "Didn't you *feel* something when you met her?"

He waited until he was in the car beside her. "Raw emotions. Confusion. One minute I'm glad—the next overwhelmed. I think Heather is lovely, but honestly during these last few weeks when I thought about our daughter, I had images of someone much younger. A child perhaps." He accelerated. "And then this beautiful young woman comes into my life and says she's my daughter. The truth is when I saw her standing there on Windy Bluff, I wanted to ask what proof she had that she belonged to me."

"What proof do you need? She looks like us, Allen. I would have known her anywhere. Didn't you feel something?"

"Dazed. Grateful. Amazed. Scared. But I'm disappointed in myself. I expected to love her on sight. Instead, I'll have to get to know her. It'll take time."

"Is that why you were so solemn out on Windy Bluff? You don't have to go this evening, Allen. I'll make some excuse."

"I promised Heather." He moved smoothly into the merging traffic. "I feel cheated out of twenty years of her life. I should have known her as a little girl, tucked her in at night and watched her grow into this lovely young woman. She would never have been adopted if I had been there."

The battle line had been drawn. "Don't say that. You weren't there—you don't know."

"I would never have given her away. And don't tell

me you were seventeen. I know how old you were. Old enough to keep her.''

"You keep forgetting—I thought you were dead.''

"Well, I'm not. All you had to do was pick up that telephone and call my father. He would have been good for another ten-thousand dollars. You could have wrung him dry. Believe me, he would have done anything for his eldest son.''

"I never spent that money.''

The car swerved. "Ah,'' he said in a mocking voice that did not sound like Allen. "So now you admit he gave you the money?''

"I never denied it—but I never spent it.''

"So what did you do with it?''

If for nothing more than a moment of peace, she told him. "I saved it. I put the money in a jewelry box along with Heather's hospital identification bracelet. It's still there.''

He jerked his head her way, his expression disbelieving. "What kind of a banking system is that? And that I.D. bracelet—that should have had my last name on it.''

"No, Allen, it had *my* last name. And I planned to give that money back to your father. But once I saw our baby I kept hoping that someday I might see her again and she would need the money.''

"You thought it might make up for leaving her?''

"Oh, Allen, I don't know what I thought. I was sick when she was born. And Mother insisted that I talk to the social worker.''

If she said anything else in her own defense, they would argue again, and arrive at the Reynard's quarreling heatedly. She folded her hands on top of her purse, crossed her legs, one high heel digging into the floorboard.

It's me, Allen, she thought. Right now I still feel like that frightened seventeen-year-old who was forced to give her baby away. But you would have an answer for that. The Kladis money. The Kladis power. The Kladis upbringing.

He wouldn't let it rest. "My parents would have taken the child. It was your duty to call my dad and ask him."

"So he could groom Heather for executive row at Larhaven? Thank goodness *that* didn't happen."

Allen had arrived at Maureen's condo this evening prepared to apologize, to ask her forgiveness for his miserable attitude. He wanted to admit the struggle he was having with the beautiful stranger called his daughter. He wanted to ask Reeny to help him sort out his feelings, his fears. Instead she was hugging the passenger side of his rental car, lost within herself, pulled into a cocoon because he had forced her there.

"I'm sorry. Really I am. This whole business has me upset."

She looked ahead, out at the traffic, her emotions in check. "Things will work out, Allen. You'll see."

Her composure amazed him, but it was a wall that shut him away. He wanted to pull to the side of the road, park there and refuse to put another mile on the odometer until they ironed out their differences. He wanted to take her in his arms, to turn back the clock with tender kisses. She would laugh out loud if she could only read his mind. Despise her? How could he despise her? Understand her? Not likely. But he wanted to stop blaming her for what had happened.

But do that, he reasoned, and I will have to blame my father, blame myself.

Right now he was too proud, too stubborn to admit

that he had failed Maureen, failed their child. He wanted to go back twenty years, to a time when it was just the two of them. Before there was a young woman named Heather.

He glanced at Maureen. Her eyes were closed. *I love you and I'm fighting it. I know it won't work out. We've dug our heels in, and we can't seem to find our way back to each other.*

It went right back to what Reeny had said the other day. They couldn't think of themselves. *Finding our daughter—knowing her—is priority.* Hadn't he said the same words?

Now that they had found her, why was he so tortured with questions? Heather *Reynard,* not Heather *Kladis.* Soon to be Heather *Martin.* He felt a fresh surge of frustration that she would never bear his name. Because of that incident in Cyprus when they thought he was dead, his name wasn't even on the birth certificate. He resented the name that she bore, resented the fact that in his mind she was still an infant.

He adjusted the knot in his tie, angry at himself for losing his cool again. Then he heard Reeny say, "We turn here. We're almost there. That's it. Heather said to park in the driveway."

It was a friendly, Spanish-style home, nice and roomy with a red-tiled roof and flower gardens in the front and the back. As she stepped from the car, Allen tucked Maureen's arm in his.

"Cozy enough?" he asked, glancing up at the front windows.

"Don't overdo it, Allen. All we have to do is be civil to each other this evening. Heather wants us to appear like friends, and I won't disappoint her."

They went up the steps and across the porch in silence. Allen jabbed the bell, but the door opened as the bell rang. He put on his best smile and knew in a flash they were overdressed. Nan Reynard was apple-cheeked and casually attired in a bright striped top with rose-colored slacks.

"Good evening, Mrs. Reynard. I hope we're not late."

"Quite early, Mr. Kladis. But dinner is almost ready."

She was a short, squat woman with a chubby face and a congenial smile. She dried her hands on an apron and extended her hands to them. "Todd," she called a little anxiously. "Our guests are here."

Todd was right behind her, peering over her shoulder through a pair of rimmed glasses that sat low on his nose. He had a ruddy complexion—a result of the heart attack Heather had mentioned?—and sandalwood hair lighter than his wife's. His gaze was guarded as he studied Allen, yet his words were friendly enough. "The children are outside running down the weeds so Nan can show you her garden after dinner."

Heather and Brett barged into the house within minutes, looking even younger than they had on Windy Bluff. Again Allen was struck at how much their daughter looked like Maureen. She had dressed in formfitting herringbone slacks with a pale yellow ribbed top as bright and chipper as her smile. She took Maureen's hands and kissed her lightly on the cheek, then grinned up at Allen.

"Hi. I'm glad you made it."

"We had no trouble at all finding you."

Brett was equally as casual in khaki shorts and a blue polo shirt. "Hey, Allen," he said, gripping his hand firmly, "you can cut the blazer and necktie if you want.

We forgot to warn you. Nan goes for relaxed meal-times.''

Allen shed his jacket, but kept his tie in place, not wanting Maureen to feel uncomfortable. Five minutes later Nan called them to the table. Allen felt hungry as a lumberjack, the aroma of pot roast and browned carrots and gravy much to his liking. As he reached for a serving platter, Maureen nudged him.

He glanced across at Heather; she winked as Todd's booming voice offered a blessing. After his faux pas, Allen waited for someone else to pick up the meat platter.

"Go on, Allen," Heather said. "The meat fork's pointing your way. And no one goes away hungry at Mom and Dad's table."

The dinner went well with Brett and Heather carrying the conversation away from touchy areas and gently steering it back to their wedding plans. Nan chatted nervously, jumping up and down every now and then to fetch something she had forgotten. Todd eased slowly into his droll sense of humor as he warmed to his guests.

"Wedding plans have been keeping us busy," he said. "Barely getting a good night's sleep anymore."

Allen rather imagined that it was more than wedding plans that had dug into Todd's sleep patterns. He recognized now that the Reynards were struggling as much as he was to make a go of this evening, and he sympathized. He feared glancing at Maureen again after seeing her eyes mist more than once during the meal.

As they finished Nan's home-baked apple pie, Allen waved off her offer of a third cup of coffee. "Heather tells us you like to chat around the table."

"Oh, we do. Do you mind? At least, let's start out here."

He wanted to take Maureen's hand and tell her that she was holding up well. She had leaned forward, her fingers entwined, her lovely face an ivory mask. He slid his hand across the back of her chair and massaged her neck.

"Allen, do you think you could wear a tuxedo on Saturday?" Todd asked.

"But—we're just guests."

"Nan has it planned out. You'll be sitting at the bridal table with us at the reception. We thought you would like that."

"You don't have to do that," Maureen said. "Just go on with the plans you've already made."

"You've been part of those plans for weeks now," Brett told them. "Nan has it all under control. Trust me."

"You just tell us what to do. What to wear. We'll be there."

Nan looked gratefully his way. Her gaze slid to Maureen now. "I'm sure you want to know all about Heather."

Maureen nodded. "Everything," she whispered. "Anything you're willing to tell us."

They laughed and cried for an hour over the antics of Heather's childhood and photos from the family albums. "We couldn't have children," Nan said, her voice cracking. "We'd been married for ten years and when we started adoption procedures, they didn't want us to take a baby."

"They thought we were too old, mind you," Todd said, rubbing his chin thoughtfully. "I may be now," he admitted, "with me pushing sixty-four like I am, but not then. We thought we had the world by the tail."

"Todd had a good job. We had this house half paid

for. We had an empty room just for Heather and an empty spot in our hearts for her to fill.''

"We'd filed all the paperwork and just kept waiting—" Todd added.

"And when we'd just about given up, the social worker called us and told us she had a three-day-old baby girl for us. Healthy as they come. Here we were— me almost forty—and about to take a little girl home. I didn't even know how to change a diaper.''

The crow's-feet around Todd's eyes crinkled. "Once we picked up that little baby, we couldn't put her down. We got the hang of diapers and baby feedings and midnight walks real fast.''

"When did you get her?" Maureen asked. "She wasn't under the Social Services long, was she? I couldn't bear it.''

"Why, no, Maureen. We called our folks that day and they flew in from New Mexico, and we went out that night and bought the crib and some baby clothes. If it hadn't been for Mother, we would have forgotten the baby formula and blankets!''

"We were really greenhorns." Todd fidgeted with his napkin. "Heather spent that first night at the social worker's home, and Nan and I paraded out in the garden all night long, wondering whether she was okay without us. We went down to the agency first thing the next morning—9:00 a.m. sharp—and picked her up.''

Nan's eyes were wet with tears. "The minute we got there, the social worker put the baby into Todd's arms. And bless his heart, he said, 'This is the most beautiful baby I ever saw.'''

She met Maureen's gaze, then Allen's. "Truth is, he hadn't seen many babies, and Heather was the first one he ever held.''

Allen ran his fingers gently down the back of Maureen's neck and felt the tiny ripple of laughter well in her throat.

"Thank you for telling us," she said. "Thank you for being so wonderful to our baby."

On Saturday Maureen sat at her dressing table in lounging pajamas, polishing her nails, her eyes aching with unshed tears. This was her daughter's wedding day and yet at two in the afternoon she would sit in the third row of the church as a guest at Heather's wedding, as a stranger in a room full of people.

She tried to picture the others, and imagined them at various tasks: Brett looking striking in his white tuxedo and breaking the speed limit trying to get to the wedding chapel in time for the photographs. The church hostess rolling out the white satin carpet down the center aisle. The florist doing a last-minute arrangement of the bouquets. Nan and Todd proud and excited as they pulled up in front of the church in a limousine. She thought bitterly of her own mother sitting stoically in her home back in Cedar Lake, curious about the ceremony, but refusing to come to her granddaughter's wedding.

Maureen's bitterness had been mellowed by her younger brother's phone call to Heather and Brett. "Wish I could be there for the big occasion," Jason had told them. "But I'll fly out later and bring my wedding gift with me."

With caution, Maureen allowed her thoughts to drift to Allen. In his hotel room, Allen would be dressing, with memories of his own marriage to Adrian.

But most of all she thought of her daughter, an hour down the Pacific Coast highway, a young bride still stretching contentedly on her bed, twirling her diamond and repeating the words Mrs. Brett Martin over and over to herself. Maureen knew that Heather would go to Brett pure, and this brought her joy in the midst of her pain.

Maureen glanced out her bedroom window. She would miss the West Coast when she moved back to Cedar Lake. This was one of those sunny California days when the beaches would be full and the ocean as calm as glass. People would be out mowing their yards and talking over the fence with neighbors. Barbecues would be smoking up the backyards, and the aroma of steaks would be filling the air. And little kids—like the one Heather had once been—would be splashing in their wading pools.

It was a lovely, happy day for a wedding.

Maureen arrived at the church at the appointed hour and found Allen waiting for her, looking handsome in his black tuxedo. He opened the car door for her.

"You're as beautiful as the bride," he said.

"You've seen her?"

"Just briefly—while they photographed the wedding party. I came a little early. I'll be going straight to the airport after the wedding."

A lump rose in her throat. She had found Heather—and was losing her to Brett. She had found Allen—and was losing him.

"Guess this is it," Allen said.

She nodded.

"You're okay, Reeny?"

"I've cried a little."

"Me, too."

"Actually I've cried a whole lot. Dwayne said it was good for the tear ducts."

"He's a good friend, Reeny. He likes you, you know."

"I know. But we can never be anything more than friends."

"He's a persistent guy."

"He's the wrong guy for me." She regretted the words but could not pull them back. "We'd better go inside before someone else takes our seats."

Allen offered his arm. She took it. "Are *you* okay, Allen?"

"Except for lack of sleep, I'm doing fine."

"I'm going on nervous energy. I called Mother again on Thursday. She still says she has no granddaughter."

"Did you tell Heather?"

"I called Nan. I couldn't face Heather with the truth. She really wanted Mother to come."

He kept her arm tight against his, and wrapped his hand around hers. "She's trying to hurt *you*, Reeny—not Heather."

"I know."

They passed through the lobby and stepped into a church sanctuary filled with guests. A trio of violins and an organ played softly—not the traditional songs or even love songs, but the glorious music of Strauss and Beethoven. She smiled. Heather and Brett were marching to the beat of their own drum. Doing things up in style.

"Friends of the bride?" the usher asked.

"Relatives of the family," Allen told him. "This is Mrs. Davenport. I'm Allen Kladis."

Maureen started to say that they were to be seated on the third row, but the usher offered her his arm. "This way," he said.

Maureen took her place beside Allen, two pews behind Nan and Todd Reynard, the Mom and Dad who

had loved and reared Heather. It was then that she tasted
the bitterness of her own salty tears. Afterwards, she
could remember only snatches of the ceremony, mostly
those things that touched her senses. The strength of Allen sitting beside her. The sweet smell of the three hundred pink and white roses with tissue-thin petals that
Allen had bought as part of their wedding present; Nan,
touched by the offer, had accepted this slight change in
her well-ordered plans.

The organ pealed out the triumphant notes of Strauss's
"One Night in Venice." The room filled with swathes
of satin and silk as the wedding party entered, the brides-
maids in scoop-neck, royal-blue gowns. An angelic
flower girl dragged behind the ring bearer who refused
to walk with her.

Brett was fidgeting until he caught sight of his bride
approaching him. Maureen leaned against Allen for
strength as they stood to watch Heather coming down
the center aisle on the arm of the man she had called
"Dad" for her lifetime. The simplicity of the bride's
dress made it more beautiful—the strapless silk taffeta
gown had a lace-trimmed bodice, a dropped waist, a long
train. And behind the veil, was the loveliest of brides.
Heather, her daughter. Heather, the bride.

Maureen listened to the preacher's words, but didn't
hear all of them. Much of the ceremony was painful for
her as she thought of how she had relinquished her hold
on "Heather" so long ago. Yet in the agony of remembering, there was joy that God in His heaven had allowed her to be here to witness her own daughter's wedding.

"Who gives this woman to this man?" the preacher
asked.

"Her mother and I do," Todd said clearly, definitely.

Inside Maureen cried out, "And Allen and I do as well."

The bride's voice was soft, barely audible, as she pledged her life, her purity and her love to her groom. Brett, with a happy grin, declared his faithfulness and love in a deep rich voice that rang through the auditorium. As they came down the aisle as Mr. and Mrs. Brett Martin, they paused to hand Nan Reynard a flower.

That should have been my flower, Maureen thought. That would have been my moment of joy if I hadn't given my baby away.

They were beside Maureen and Allen now. A tiny smile touched Heather's lips as she met Maureen's gaze. In an impulsive gesture, Brett reached over and squeezed Allen's shoulder.

Afterwards, Maureen could not remember driving to the reception at the waterfront hotel. She knew only that she had a valet parking ticket in her purse. In spite of Allen's urging, she barely touched the buffet dinner and felt sudden apprehension when Todd Reynard asked Allen to toast the bride and groom.

Allen stood in the center of the room and lifted his goblet of sparkling cider toward Brett and Heather. "Heather, Maureen and I have known you for such a little while," he said, "but long enough to know that you are beautiful like your mother."

Maureen held her breath. Nan grasped Todd's hand.

"And you, Brett—you are young, but you have a strong faith and a deep commitment to your bride. You have grown up in homes full of love. But Maureen and I are more aware of how much Nan and Todd have sacrificed to bring Heather to this special day. We salute them and you on this, your wedding day. Take good care of her, Brett. Your bride is accustomed to being treated with great gentleness and deep affection. We wish you the same abundance of love and happiness that Nan and Todd have showered on your bride until this day."

Allen lifted the goblet and saluted them.

Moments later Brett and Heather took to the black marble dance floor with such grace that Maureen marveled. Later still, Brett stood at her side, asking, "Maureen, may I?"

As he guided her gracefully across the shiny black marble, she did not hear what Brett said, nor even know whether he formed words at all. She had glanced over his shoulder to her daughter, dancing in the arms of Allen, her small white-gloved hand in his. She had grown up never seeing either one of them, never knowing them, and yet her quick easy smile, the tilt of her chin as she gazed up at Allen, the turn of her head, the brilliant dark eyes were Allen all over again. And her flare for independence, for setting goals, her love of classical music, her willingness to chart a different course, if need be— these she inherited from Maureen.

After the reception—after the dancing—after the bride and groom drove away, Allen walked Maureen back to valet parking. The attendant dashed off for her sports car.

"It went well, Maureen. Better than I had hoped for."

"You didn't mind being introduced at the reception?"

There were lights in the arched driveway, but he kept his face in the shadows. "Did they really have to turn everyone's attention on us that way? I felt a bit self-conscious being introduced as Heather's birth father."

"But you *are* her birth father."

The arrival of Maureen's shiny car delayed Allen's answer. He handed the attendant his own parking ticket and then tipped him generously. "Being introduced like that was humiliating, Reeny."

It had been a painful experience for Maureen, too, but she felt relieved when the whole room received them warmly.

She slipped behind the steering wheel and looked at Allen through the open window. "I'm sorry it embarrassed you."

"I felt like a failure as a father—like I'd let Heather down. I have so much to learn."

"We both do, but we have time."

He nodded. "I'm counting on that. When I danced with Heather and when I said good-bye to her, I told her how proud I was."

"Were you?"

"Yes. I told you I always wanted a daughter. And as I watched her standing up front in that church—looking so beautiful and so much like you—I knew in my heart that she was my daughter. I accepted her as my own that moment." He stared up at the stars. "I know that I'm really going to love that girl. I already do."

Maureen felt her happiness at his confession mixed with regret. Even now, as they were saying goodbye, she wished that Allen could love her as well. She swallowed the lump in her throat and turned the key in the ignition.

"Are you flying out tonight?"

"If I get to the airport in time. I still have to get out of this tuxedo and turn in my car. I'm cutting it close."

"You could have slipped away early."

"No, I promised Heather I'd be there for the whole show."

"Take care of yourself, Allen," she said huskily.

"You, too."

Allen stepped back as she drove away, her tires squealing. Maureen did not glance in the rearview mirror. She had to drive away before she cried. The ache inside was unbearable. Ironic, she thought, Allen and I are going our separate ways on the very day that our daughter has realized her greatest happiness.

Chapter Twenty

Knowing that Allen would take the freeway, Maureen drove down the less-traversed, darkened Pacific Coast highway. During the daylight hours, the road was often bumper-to-bumper, but now at the midnight hour only the lights of a few cars glared in her rearview mirror.

She lowered the window, letting in more of the sea breeze, and rested her elbow on the sill. To her left, the breakers crashed against the shore, wave after wave beating against the pilings at the pier. She counted three or four beach fires with the darkened silhouettes of beach-goers gathered around them.

The beach. It brought back memories of Allen.

She considered walking on the sand, but she was on a darker stretch of the roadway, a lonely area where it would be unwise for a woman to roam about at night.

She resigned herself to heading straight home. Home to nothing. There was nothing left. She had found her daughter, but they could never be more than friends. She had found Allen again, but he obviously did not care for her as she cared for him.

The certified letter from Larhaven remained on her desk, unopened—her termination notice and she hadn't even read the terms. Her job at Fabian was all but ended. But she refused to be a quitter. She had driven herself for years in a corporate treadmill. Now she was ready for a fresh start. She would put her condo up for sale, pack up and go back to Cedar Lake where she grew up. Not to Anderson, where two of her brothers lived and where her mother often visited, but back to something familiar.

She turned down the street to her condo, dark except for the streetlights. A car sat in the No Parking zone. A tall, familiar figure with his hands in his pockets leaned against it.

She eased her car forward and leaned out the window. "Dwayne? What are you doing here?"

He grinned, his gray eyes behind the glasses looking black in the darkness. "I thought you might need a friend. Thought you might be feeling a big letdown after the wedding and with Allen taking off."

In the past few weeks, Dwayne had become the confidant of both Maureen and Allen, sharing in their search to find Heather. Though there was still much he didn't know, especially about her relationship with Allen, Maureen reflected.

"Yes, Allen is on his way to Seattle."

"Then how about some coffee and conversation? You make the coffee, I'll do the rest."

It seemed unkind to make excuses, but her strength was sapped. "Dwayne, I'm tired. It's been a long day."

"A tough day?"

"A long, tough day," she admitted. "But beautiful."

"So are you with the moonlight touching your face."

She looked up. The moon peered over the palm trees. Stars that she could never name glittered above them.

"Now the moonbeams are making your eyes sparkle, Maureen."

She laughed. "You'd better go home and get some sleep."

"Not until I see you safely inside."

"Then let me put my car away for the night."

He touched her shoulder. "Let me go with you."

"The garage is gated. It's safe."

"Just move over, Maureen."

As she slid across, he took the driver's seat. He sniffed. "Smells like a florist shop in here."

"I brought three of the table bouquets home with me."

After parking the car, he helped her carry the flowers up to the condo, spilling water on the way. Once inside, Maureen kicked off her shoes and removed her earrings. "Sit down, Dwayne," she invited.

He sat on the edge of the sofa cushion, his fingers locked, moving nervously. "Is Allen ever coming back?"

"On business trips."

"That won't include you?"

"I rather think not. Unless they deal with missiles."

"Did things go well this evening?" he asked.

"We got along just fine. We did it for Heather."

Dwayne picked up the framed photo of Heather taken on the bluffs the day she met Maureen. "You have a beautiful daughter."

Maureen's eyes misted. She slipped into her recliner and curled her legs under her. "I never thought I'd see her again, Dwayne. Thanks for putting us in touch with the social worker. For helping us out that way."

"I told you, I'm here when you need me."

"I appreciate your friendship."

"I'd like to be more," he said evenly. "But I can wait. You are worth waiting for, Maureen."

She eyed him. When you're not calculating figures, she thought, you're a kind man, Dwayne. He would make a good companion. But she said, "I'm going away, Dwayne. Once I get my desk packed up and this condo sold—"

"But your job at Fabian is good for another six weeks."

"But I'm ready for a fresh start."

"Do you have some place in mind?"

"I'm going back to the Lake County south of Chicago."

Should she name the place, risk him coming to see her? What harm would it do? "I'm getting homesick for Cedar Lake, Indiana."

"I thought *this* was home." He leaned forward, his body stooped in weariness. "Will you be happy there, Maureen?"

"I hope so."

She shrugged, thinking about the tranquillity of the lake, and slipping away on Sunday mornings with her dad to go fishing or hiking among the cedar trees, or picnicking in the parks with her friends. She thought about those long hours of childhood, browsing at the library, reading about a bigger world out there that she wanted to know, wanted to see. She had taken a bite out of living, but she recognized now that life had been happy until the family moved to California when she was a freshman in high school. After that, things had not gone well—not with her father dying. Not until she met Allen.

"Dwayne, is anyone ever really happy?" she asked.

"Your daughter is."

She wet her lips. "Yes. Yes, I believe she is."

"Maureen, there's no aircraft industry in Cedar Lake."

"Chicago is only a few miles away. I'll find work there."

"You're an ambitious woman—only a fool would toss away her education and experience as a scientific researcher."

"I'll only set those things aside for a time, but not forever. Ambition doesn't die with disappointment."

"That position at the Pentagon is yours at the bat of an eye, Maureen," he reminded her.

"But I see no need to rush into another job right now."

He plucked his glasses from his face and rubbed his eyes. "Will you be all right—financially, I mean?"

"Allen guaranteed a three-month severance pay. That, with my own investments and savings, should carry me over for a while."

He looked up now and met her gaze, his gray eyes pensive. "I could take care of you if you would let me."

"Oh, Dwayne, that wouldn't work out."

"It would if you gave it a chance."

"But...I'm not in love with you."

If her reply had hurt him, he didn't show it. "Just my luck. Will I see you again?"

"At Fabian. At the conference table."

"I mean for dinner. Just the two of us."

"Maybe before I move back to Cedar Lake."

He squinted as he put his glasses on again. "What does Cedar Lake have that I can't give you?"

"Tranquillity. Peace. Memories. I grew up there, you

know. I want to go back and buy a small place of my own. Get active in one of the small community churches—give God a chance in my life."

"Wow. You have changed."

"I just *need* a change." Most of all, she would try to reconcile with her mother. And with her God. And after that, she would think about what she really wanted to do with the rest of her life.

His tone turned brusque. "You've just met your daughter. Are you really going to move away and lose touch with her again?"

"Oh, Dwayne, she doesn't need me."

"I think you're wrong."

"I don't want to interfere in her life."

"So you're going to walk out on her again—just like that?"

She winced. "I think you'd better leave now. It really has been an exhausting day."

He stood, his hands in his pockets, his droll sense of humor gone. "Maureen, you would never forgive yourself for going away again. Sort it out. Separate that beautiful young daughter from your feelings toward Allen."

"How can I?" she whispered. "Allen is her father."

He tugged at his earlobe. "Tell me to back off if I'm nosing in, but Allen told me his father paid you to go away—that's why you never got together twenty years ago."

"That's not true. Not completely. Allen's father wanted me to go away all right—so Allen would never know about Heather."

"What a cheap thing to do."

"It was ten thousand dollars, Dwayne."

He whistled. "I'd take a long trip, too."

"My mother took the money from him. I never

wanted it. As much as I despised Allen's father, he thought he was doing what was best."

"Protecting his son from his responsibility?"

"Allen didn't know about Heather."

"Why didn't you tell him? I would have called the navy. The Red Cross. Anything—so Allen would own up to his responsibility."

"I wrote to him—but never mailed the letter." Even after all this time, her voice caught. "That's when the navy reported Allen dead. All I had left was ten-thousand dollars in my jewelry box. I was too heartsick to think about it, and later, too proud to mail it back." She smiled ruefully. "The truth is, I didn't want his parents to know about the baby—"

"But they knew."

"Yes. His father suspected I was pregnant, but I was afraid that with Allen gone, they might try to claim her."

"Wouldn't it have been better for the family to keep her?"

"It didn't seem so to me at the time. It still doesn't. Funny, Dwayne, I kept that money—never spent it—hoping that I could one day give it to Heather. Does that make sense?"

"Better than letting it mold in your jewelry box."

"Brett and Heather will need money—what with Brett still in seminary. I'm going to set up a savings account for them."

"That's a pretty hefty wedding present. You're a re-markable woman, Maureen."

A lonely woman, she thought.

He walked across the room, leaned down and kissed her on the cheek. "I can help you pack up if you're determined to go."

"You're sweet."

"I'm just trying to impress you—just in case." He straightened, tall and wiry, his sensitive mouth turned down. "You know, I despise Allen Kladis and I envy him all at the same time."

"Why? What has he ever done to you?"

"Hurt you. He doesn't realize how much you love him—how much he's walked out on. You'll be carrying your torch for him all the way back to Cedar Lake."

"That's foolishness."

"That's what I've been trying to tell both of you." His grin was little more than a crooked twist of his lips. "Don't get up. I'll see myself out, Maureen."

Familiar words, she thought. Allen's words.

Too tired to get up to turn out the lights and go to bed, she dozed in the recliner. She awakened a few minutes later with someone knocking at her door. Was Dwayne back?

As the knock persisted, her heart beat in her throat again. Had Dwayne locked the door behind him? She lurched from the recliner, stumbling as she reached the door and peered through the peephole.

She yanked the door open. "Allen, how did you get into the building?"

"Dwayne let me in as he left."

She pushed her hair from her face and stepped back so he could enter. He dropped his briefcase by the door.

"I don't understand. What are you doing here? Did you miss the plane?"

"I forgot something important, Maureen."

"What?"

"You."

He towered above her, the lamplight casting shadows on his handsome face, his dark eyes moving over her.

His deep voice held steady as he said, "I was at the airport. Already checked in. But I couldn't leave without you, Reeny. I didn't find you after all these years to let you go."

She tried to clear her thoughts, wondering for a moment if she might be dreaming. Was Allen only a mirage, an optical illusion, a phantom taunting her? No, she was not imagining. He was here, real, full of life. "What are you saying, Allen?"

"I'm saying, I won't leave without you."

"We've hardly gotten along these last few days."

"I know. That's my fault. I've been fighting these old feelings—my attraction to you."

"It seemed more like you were fighting *me*."

He nodded, remorse stealing across his expression. "I've kept my emotions in check for a year now. Denied my own needs. Buried them. And then I saw you again and felt some of the old stirrings. I kept telling myself, 'This is just physical longing. You can't hurt Reeny again.' I was running scared, Reeny, so I pushed you away so you wouldn't know how I was feeling."

"I felt the same way," she said in a small voice. "That's why I came up to Seattle. And then everything seemed to go wrong. I knew that nothing good could come unless you knew about our daughter. I thought Adrian stood in our way. But it was Heather."

"When you told me about the baby, I felt betrayed—betrayed by the very woman I loved."

Her words were barely audible. "Allen, I was so afraid you would walk out on me if I told you the truth. I kept putting it off. Kept thinking, why would it matter when I didn't even know where she was? But I hated myself for not telling you—"

"What happened to you was my fault. I only wish I

had been there for you. Been there for our baby. Can you ever forgive me?''

She touched her fingers to his lips. "It's okay. It's over. Everything worked out the best for her."

''That's what she told me when we danced together... And she asked me whether I was running out on you again.''

"She asked you that?"

"She said I'd be a fool to let you go again. She's very, very special—like her mother. But what about us? Did it work out the best for us?'' He pressed her fingers against his lips and kissed them. "I still love you, Reeny. I just didn't know how to tell you. I didn't trust my own feelings.''

Neither one of them moved. Twenty years slipped into oblivion. Yesterday became today. This moment. And then they were in each other's arms, Allen holding her so tightly that she knew he would never let her go again.

''Say something, Reeny.''

She lifted her face to him. "I don't know what to say.''

''How about 'I love you' for starters?''

She dissolved into tears of joy. He wiped them away, his thumb gliding gently across her cheek. He caressed her, kissed her again—her earlobe, her throat, her lips. "I love you, Reeny. I want you to marry me.''

It was not how Maureen planned it. They were not out on a rocky bluff with the moon full or with a perfect sunset over the Pacific. But here they were in her condo at three in the morning with sunrise still hours away. Her hair was a mess, her clothes rumpled, her shoes kicked off...

''Look at me, Allen. I'm a sight.''

''I'm looking, and you're beautiful.''

She began to laugh. "Do you know what?"

"What?" he asked.

"Your hair looks as tousled and windblown as the day I met you. I can still picture you balancing that crazy surfboard in one hand and a milk shake in the other."

"Crazy? Is that what you thought of me?"

"No, I thought you were the most handsome boy I'd ever met."

"And now?"

"I feel the same way... I feel something special every time I look at you. I love you, Allen. I have always loved you." She met his gaze, anxious to know for certain. "But it's not just Heather's wedding, is it? Will you feel this way tomorrow?"

"The wedding was just the catalyst. But I didn't *need* the wedding. I felt this way twenty years ago. I still do.... Will you marry me, Reeny?"

She barely had time to say yes. Then his warm lips came down hard on hers, the tangy scent of his cologne engulfing them.

Later, as she caught her breath, he said, "I don't want a big wedding like Heather had. Just a simple one."

"I'd like that."

"But we will have to wait until Heather and Brett get back from their honeymoon."

"Why?"

His eyes twinkled. "So they can stand up for us."

Chapter Twenty-One

❧

On a glorious September morning, Maureen and Allen were married at the Wayfarer's Chapel, high on a bluff overlooking the Pacific Ocean. They kept their wedding plans uncomplicated, informal. Maureen dressed in a lovely summer frock, a powder-blue chiffon with a heart-shaped bodice and a skirt that swirled gracefully around her knees; she carried a small bouquet with three red roses. Allen wore a new blue suit with a red rosebud in his buttonhole, and the silk tie his daughter had given him.

Before the ceremony, they walked through the Azalea Gardens while they waited for their turn in the chapel. They walked alone, just the two of them, arm in arm. They strolled to the edge of the bluff to look down in silence on the beach and the ocean. And then with Maureen's arm in Allen's, they walked back toward the bell tower and the gold-leaf cross that rose high above the chapel.

Allen squeezed her hand. "They call that cross God's Candle. At least that's what the sailors at sea call it."

They paused before entering the chapel, as the Wayfarer's welcome had invited them to do, and felt that uplifting of their spirits, an awareness of God. Maureen reached up and straightened Allen's tie. "No regrets?" she asked.

"No regrets."

He leaned down and kissed the curve of her ear and sang the words from a favorite song of his. And then he said, "Reeny, the promises I'm about to make to you in the chapel, I've already made in my heart. I want you as my life's companion. I want you always."

Maureen had never loved Allen more. Nor had she ever seen him look more handsome. Smile lines formed around his mouth. His dark eyes danced like the shimmering lights on the water. And yet there was that serious, gentle look about him and the strength that his height and broad shoulders imparted. She could see by his expression that he was a happy man.

She smiled up at him.

Then hand in hand they walked into the tiny chapel where the redwood pillars formed an arch above the sanctuary. Maureen felt sheltered by its walls, comforted by its beauty. Sky and trees. Stone and glass. Light and nature. Architectural patterns intricately woven together. They seemed to be stepping over a floor of diamonds and looking up at a sky-blue ceiling, its colors so delicate that it looked like fleecy clouds above them. Steps led up to the altar. Mountain water bubbled to the surface at the baptismal font. Gilded letters formed the opening words of "The Lord's Prayer."

Our Father, Maureen thought. He has given us all of this.

Together they went toward the altar where Brett and Heather waited for them. Their other guests smiled as they passed, but Nan Reynard's smile turned to tears. She grabbed a handkerchief from Todd and dabbed at her eyes. Maureen's mother was visibly absent, but Maureen's younger brother Jason had flown out to wish them well, and she was grateful to him. Nick seemed a happy guest as he cast a proud glance at the five restless children beside him. Fran slid her hand into Nick's. And Chris, with the flight plans in his back pocket, winked at Maureen. Seated in the back pew was Dwayne Crocker. Seeing Dwayne sitting there with his eyes downcast, Maureen whispered a quick prayer that God would bring Dwayne the same happiness that was hers today.

Even though it was early morning, the candles were lit. An open Bible lay on the altar. A friend of Brett's, a pleasant-faced clergyman in a long, flowing robe, stood behind it. The chapel organist played as they came forward, and with the light streaming through the windows they exchanged their wedding vows. The ceremony was brief and when it ended, the clarion bell in the tower chimed.

As they stepped from the chapel back into the sunshine, Allen asked, "Well, how does it feel to be Mrs. Allen Kladis?"

"Perfect. Just perfect."

The wedding party drove from Rancho Palos Verdes back into Beverly Hills for a private brunch at the Regent Hotel. At the last bite and the last toast, Heather asked, "Maureen, where are you honeymooning?"

She shrugged and nodded toward Allen. "It's a total secret. He won't tell me."

But Chris seemed to know, because as Allen and Maureen left the others standing in the hotel's vaulted lobby, Chris followed them out to the limousine.

"L.A. International," Chris told the driver.

"Flight number?" the driver asked.

"Not important."

Allowing the newlyweds some privacy, Chris settled himself in the far corner and dozed until they reached the airport.

"Where are we going, Allen? To Alaska?" Maureen asked.

He winked mischievously. "You'll find out soon enough. It's a special place for a very special lady." He laughed, and cupped her chin, kissing her again, smothering any other questions.

When they reached the airport, Chris directed the driver past the main terminal to the private landing strip where the Larhaven company jet was waiting for them.

"We're flying in that?" Maureen asked.

"Why not?" Chris asked. "I've already filed my flight plan."

"Will we get where we're going?"

"With Chris in the cockpit," Allen said, "there's no problem."

"That's right. We'll fuel along the way if we need to, Maureen." And he went about helping her on board, whistling.

In the early evening, their plane touched down at a small airstrip across the Canadian border. Chris unloaded their luggage, and then, grinning, hugged Maureen and thumped his big brother on the shoulder.

"I'll see you two again in ten days."

"It's late. You're sure you don't want to over-night?" Allen asked, concerned.

"Hey, it's your honeymoon. You don't want your kid brother tagging along. Don't worry about me. I'll be home in an hour.'' With a quick wink, Chris was back on board, preparing to leave. They watched until he was airborne and the company plane a mere speck in the sky, winging its way around the bends of the lake and disappearing between the mountain ridges.

Maureen shivered in the crisp mountain air and snuggled into her cashmere. ''I'll freeze without a coat, Allen.''

''I had Heather pack some warm clothes for you. And if they're not enough, I'll have something flown over from one of the shops in Vancouver.''

She glanced around. Even in the early dusk, the craggy, tree-covered Coastal Mountains of British Columbia—snow-capped already—rose in tiers around the pristine lake. To the right, a secluded blue lagoon rippled against the shore.

''It's beautiful, Allen.''

''It's called Harrison Hot Springs. One of my favorite places. I knew you would like it. It's a place to remember.''

Any place with you will be a place to remember, she thought.

As they turned to the taxi, she breathed in the fresh, clear air, scented with evergreens and sweet-smelling autumn flowers. Their taxi moved leisurely up the Esplanade, the narrow village road along the glistening lake, past weeping shade trees with pear-shaped leaves and around the curved drive to the Harrison Hotel. Two bellhops were at the door to welcome them.

''Mr. and Mrs. Allen Kladis,'' Allen told the receptionist.

Her eyes twinkled. ''Oh, you're on the honeymoon package.''

''On an extended one.''

"Have a wonderful time at the Harrison. We've reserved a table for you in the Copper Room," she said as he finished signing the registry. "Unless you want to have room service."

"No," Allen said. "My wife promised me one dance on our wedding night. If you could have the bellhop take our things to the room, I think we'll go straight on to dinner."

"Allen, I look a mess!" Maureen protested.

He tipped the bellhop generously and then met her worried gaze. "You look elegant to me." He reached out and flicked a strand of tawny hair behind her ear. "I love you, Mrs. Kladis."

Afterward, Maureen could not remember what she ordered or whether she even finished what was set before her. All she remembered was the subdued earthtones and the golden glow of the dining room, and the sweetness of dancing in Allen's arms.

Hand in hand they took the elevator up to the honeymoon suite. Unlocking the door, Allen swept her into his arms again and carried her across the threshold. She blushed with pleasure at finding him so traditional, so romantic.

The room boasted a magnificent view of the lake. A king-size bed sat in the middle of the room with a hot tub steps away. Pink candles and souvenir goblets were on the round table with the hotel's Honeymoon Certificate beside them. A massive bouquet of roses and carnations and a deluxe fruit basket had been placed on the dresser top. Allen undid his tie while he dialed the operator a second time and said, "Hold all our calls until further notice."

Maureen disappeared into the dressing room to unpack. When she finally emerged, the bathroom lights glowed against the wall, shadow-mirroring her as she stood there. She listened. Silence. Had Allen stepped out? Fallen asleep waiting for her? But, no, the Do Not Disturb sign was no longer hanging inside the doorknob. The double latch had been secured, the lights in the room lowered.

She peered around the door frame, and saw Allen standing by the wide windows with the thick flowered curtains drawn back. He stood motionless, his broad muscular back to her. He stood tall, pensive as he stared out on the lake—so deep in thought.

Maureen snapped off the light switch, putting the dressing room in darkness. As she drew closer, Allen continued to gaze out on the lake, his back still to her, his ear seemingly deaf to her coming. She realized now that the candles on the round table had been lit. They flickered against the crystal goblets imprinted with their names and this date: their wedding day. A bottle of sparkling cider lay in an iced bucket beside them. And propped up against Allen's shaving kit, she saw the blue Honeymoon Certificate. She had already memorized the words: This certificate has been presented to Mr. and Mrs. Allen Kladis on the occasion of their honeymoon while staying at the Harrison Hot Springs Hotel in Harrison Hot Springs, B.C., Canada.

Her heart skipped a beat. These little touches were Allen's doing. But his silence worried her.

"Allen, are you all right?"

"I heard you coming," he said, but he did not turn. "You look beautiful."

"How would you know?"

"I've been watching your reflection in the window glass and thinking what a lucky man I am."

He turned now and held out his arm to draw her to

him. "I love you, Reeny. I can't undo the lost years, but I promise you the rest of my life. And I couldn't give you Cedar Lake, but I'm giving you The Harrison."

"You've been here before?"

"Never with anyone important," he replied, erasing her sudden concern that he'd been here with Adrian.

His grip tightened as he pressed her head against his chest. She felt his strength, his nearness, as they stood with their bodies touching, and felt his strong heartbeat against her cheek. She heard laughter in his voice as he hummed the song that he had sung to her outside the Wayfarer's Chapel. Gently he said, "That's what I want, Reeny—you for my life's companion. This is for keeps, sweetheart. I plan to spend the rest of my life with you— to even grow old with you."

Outside, the night sky was a canopy of stars with fleecy white clouds clinging to the mountaintops. But what she felt was the stillness. Utter stillness. Serenity. There was no buzz of city traffic. No noisy crowds. Just a quiet village with no phones ringing. No bitter memories entangling them. From their windows, she could see the lake water lapping against the boats and the rocks, and could almost feel the September wind rippling the surface. She had never been happier. Here, alone with Allen, all she heard was the deep rhythmic sound of his breathing, the steady beat of his heart, the wild thumping of her own. The longing and desire to be completely Allen's welled with rising intensity inside her.

Allen turned, filled their crystal goblets with sparkling cider and handed one to her. He touched her glass with his; they sipped. He left the drapes drawn, let the beauty of their surroundings fill the room. Then he blew the candles out and with his arm tightly around her waist, they went toward the king-size bed. Willingly, gladly they moved toward the perfect fulfilling of their wedding vows—and to the sealing of that promise to love each other forever that they had made so long ago on the white sandy beach beneath the Huntington Beach Pier.

Epilogue

May 10, Mother's Day, Seattle

As Allen showered, Maureen Kladis moved through the newly decorated living room past the mantel with their wedding picture on one end and their daughter's picture on the other. They had been married two years.

After spending a memorable ten-day honeymoon in Canada, they had flown home to Seattle, where Maureen settled into her new job as part of executive row at Larhaven. She was just two doors from her husband's spacious office, hers equally impressive.

At first they clashed over procedures in the aircraft industry and had real rows over staying in Allen's condo. But being the practical woman that she was, she realized how happy Allen was living in a place that overlooked Lake Washington. She loved it herself. She recanted. They bartered. Finally Allen agreed to her terms. In five years he planned to retire early—freeing them to move on. In the meantime, she would redecorate the entire place—drapes, furniture and all—and even order new appliances and an ivory countertop for the compact kitchen. And she would definitely replace the photos on the mantelpiece.

Weeks later, Allen never said a word—he couldn't—when he walked into his refurbished study and found Adrian's pictures on the bookshelf. He flashed Reeny a grateful smile.

"She's part of your life, Allen. Always will be."

"But it's not fair to you—"

"Let them stay there as long as you need them."

He nodded gratefully. "I'm a very lucky man," he said.

"I am lucky too," she replied.

You love us both, she thought. In different ways.

Within a month, she noticed a framed photo of herself in its place. Allen had released Adrian and embraced Reeny. And none of this would have come to pass if it hadn't been for you, Heather dear, Maureen thought.

She glanced lovingly at the gold-framed picture of Heather on the fireplace mantel. So utterly guileless, innocent in her smile, genuine in her actions.

Joy flooded Maureen.

So much had happened in these last two years. Everything seemed perfect... Except for you, Mama, she thought sadly. You still have not forgiven us. You still refuse to make us part of your family again. I can understand not allowing Allen and me back into your life. But Heather is your grandchild, Mother. She wants to know you.

Reeny turned from the fireplace, more determined than ever, and made her way to the ancient escritoire in the corner of the room. Sitting down, she reached for a fresh sheet of writing paper. As she took a pen from the rolltop pigeonhole, she felt suddenly at peace. She was confident that one day soon, very soon, her mother would come around.

Dear Mother,

In just moments, Allen will tell me to hurry. He doesn't like going to church late, not since we joined that large congregation in Bellevue. We don't know many people yet, but sitting there Sunday after Sunday, we feel the warmth and welcome of those around us.

Even though we are pressed for time, I just had to write. I had to tell you how happy I am. Today was one of the happiest days of my life. Heather called me, almost at the crack of dawn.

She woke us up, and Allen handed me the phone, saying groggily, "It's our daughter."

Our daughter. Do you hear that, Mom? Our daughter. *My daughter.*

"Darling, is anything wrong?" I cried.

"No, of course not. I just called to wish you a happy Mother's Day—*Mother.*"

Mother.

Oh, Mom, I burst into tears. The drapes were open. I could see Lake Washington through the sliding glass doors. It was so peaceful. So beautiful. The water barely rippling. A sailboat skimming along just beneath our bedroom window. The sun forming rainbows across the water. Bringing rainbows to my heart. Not a sound outside except for the song of a robin.

And the music inside—my daughter calling me *Mother.*

It was the first time.

"What's wrong?" Allen asked me. "Is Heather okay?"

I hushed him with my finger to my lips. Not wanting to hear another sound except that word *Mother*.

From the beginning we had agreed that Nan and Todd Reynard were her parents, her mom and dad. We could never take their place. Mom, I gave birth to Heather, but they were the ones who loved her and brought her up to be such a charming young woman. Early on we all agreed that it was best for Heather to call us by our given names. Allen. Maureen. Once or twice she even called me Reeny the way Allen does. But today, for the first time, she called me "Mother." And I shall float on that memory and the sweetness of that word until my dying day.

Mother, I wish you were home and not off on a camping trip with my brothers or fishing there on Cedar Lake like we used to do with Dad. Oh, I want you to have fun and know that you are. But I want so much to hear your voice and to talk with you and tell you how happy I am. And I would like so much to tell you "Happy Mother's Day."

I've caused you so much pain and shame over the years. I've tried to make up for it. Top grades at the university. Success in my career. And those deposits in your bank account month after month. Did you not wonder who sent them? I sent them, Mom. I didn't want you to struggle the way you did after Daddy died. None of those things matter now, but, oh Mother, when you ignored the invitation to the wedding when Allen and I married— that hurt.

How long must we wait for your approval? You still sound so distant when we call you. And your little one-page notes in answer to our letters seem so inadequate. But I think you are warming up to us now, saying more. I want so much to have your forgiveness. Allen longs for it even more. We have God's forgiveness and peace. But we want yours as well. Won't you change your mind and come and spend some time with us?

Come this summer when Heather is here. Allen and I will be celebrating our second wedding anniversary soon—and so will Heather and Brett. Your granddaughter so wants to meet you. You would like her. There is such a sweetness about her. Perhaps that sounds like no one you know in the Birkland family, but Nan and Todd Reynard are like that. Kind-hearted people. So much of them shines through Heather.

Summer is coming—almost here. But if you won't come this summer—you spoke of so many plans with the boys—what about Christmas? You and Heather and I can shop till we drop. Mother, please, say you'll come.

The condo is totally redecorated and the spare bedrooms ready for guests. Heather and Brett will use one, but you would love the smaller room. It's very private with a bath and veranda of its own that looks out on the lake.

Nan and Todd insisted that Heather spend this Christmas with Allen and me—the very first one away from them. The very first one with us. Nan and Todd feel we need that holiday time with her. We invited them to come too—even promised to put them up in a hotel—but they refused. "Some other time,'' Nan told us.

Brett is a dear boy and ever so swallowed up in the Good Book. That's right. We have a preacher of our own now in his first pastorate in a small rural village.

I've saved the best news to last. Heather and Brett are expecting their first child in early January. Maybe the baby will come for Christmas. Like Heather and Brett, Allen and I are beside ourselves with pleasure. We won't have to vie for position with the baby. Nan and Todd and Allen and I have all agreed that the four of us will make marvelous grandparents.

I am so ready to hold a baby in my arms. I let one baby go. You begged me to do so for the sake of the family. But for more than twenty years, it has torn us apart. Now God in His goodness has given us back our lives with the added promise of a grandchild of our own. Your first great-grandchild, Mother, as Heather was your first grandchild. Come, please. Come and be part of all that has happened to us these last two years.

Maureen leaned back and reread the letter, tears blurring her vision. Satisfied, she folded it and tucked it in the scented envelope. As she licked the flap and applied the stamp, she heard Allen coming quietly over the thick carpet behind her.

"Better hurry," he said as she faced him.

"All I need to do is slip on the new dress you gave me. But can we mail my letter on the way?"

He glanced at his watch. "Is it that important?"

"It's a letter to Mother. I told her about Heather's

call." She blinked back the tears. "And I asked her to forgive us—"

"Again?" He sighed. "She will, honey. We just have to give your mother time."

"I've already given her twenty years."

"If we have to, Maureen, we'll give her another twenty." He cupped her chin, his mouth curving into a loving smile.

He glanced at his watch again. "Okay, we'll drop your letter off at the post office. But get a move on you."

"Why all the hurry, Allen?"

"We have to be to church on time. This is the morning they pass out a carnation to every mother present."

"Oh, Allen."

He held out his hand and pulled her to her feet. She went into his arms willingly and lingered there, her cheek pressed against his. For a moment she wished that they could stay home. Just the two of them. But, no, that would be so ungrateful when they had so much to be thankful for.

Then she heard his throaty ripple, "I am so lucky. You have made me a happy man, Reeny."

She tilted her face toward him, smiling. "You're special, too," she told him.

"I love you. Always have. Always will," he said. Then just before his lips met hers, his dark eyes brightened. "Happy Mother's Day, Reeny."

* * * * *

Dear Reader,

Books are my personal friends, the nooks of a library my refuge, the privilege of writing novels the fulfillment of a childhood goal. Books challenged me with impossible dreams like attending West Point or Annapolis decades before women were admitted to their hallowed halls. I worked side by side with Nancy Drew solving the mysteries of hidden staircases and caves. And Heidi never climbed the Alps without me panting on the slopes beside her. Books have remained my companions for a lifetime.

As a nurse, I was tenderized by people in search of themselves, in search of health and answers regarding their families and careers, their life and eternal life. Maureen Davenport, the heroine of this novel, has successfully climbed the corporate ladder, but she grieves for a lost love and cannot put a face to the child she gave up for adoption; the hero searches for peace as a widower; and a young woman down the Pacific Coast searches for her birth parents. All three find that the human heart also has the capacity for eternity—a search that offers lasting peace in a personal acquaintance with a living God and a loving Savior.

In your own search for answers for your career and future, your family and friends, your health and leisure, God is there to brighten your day, ease your maddening rush, comfort your sadness and to guide you over crooked paths as He brings you through the tough and good times with joy and gladness.

In friendship,

Doris Elaine Fell